Princess Academy

Princess Academy

SHANNON HALE

SCHOLASTIC INC.
New York Toronto London Auckland Sydney
Mexico City New Delhi Hong Kong Buenos Aires

ISBN-13: 978-0-439-88811-0
ISBN-10: 0-439-88811-5

Published by Scholastic Inc., 557 Broadway, New York, NY 10012,
by arrangement with Bloomsbury Children's Books USA.

12 11 10 9 8 7 6 5 4 3 2 1 6 7 8 9 10 11/0

Printed in the U.S.A. 40

First Scholastic printing, September 2006

Typeset in Weiss

For good friends

And especially for Rosi,
a true mountain girl

Chapter One

The east says it's dawn
My mouth speaks a yawn
My bed clings to me and begs me to stay
I hear a work song
Say winter is long
I peel myself up and then make away

Miri woke to the sleepy bleating of a goat. The world was as dark as eyes closed, but perhaps the goats could smell dawn seeping through the cracks in the house's stone walls. Though still half-asleep, she was aware of the late autumn chill hovering just outside her blanket, and she wanted to curl up tighter and sleep like a bear through frost and night and day.

Then she remembered the traders, kicked off her blanket, and sat up. Her father believed today was the day their wagons would squeeze up the mountain pass and rumble into the village. This time of year, all the villagers felt the rush for the last trading of the season, to hurry and square off a few more linder blocks and make that much more to trade, that much more to eat during the snow-locked months. Miri longed to help.

Wincing at the rustle of her pea-shuck mattress, Miri stood and stepped carefully over her pa and older sister, Marda, asleep on their pallets. For a week she had harbored an anxious hope to run to the quarry today and be already at work when her pa arrived. Perhaps then he might not send her away.

She pulled her wool leggings and shirt over her sleep clothes, but she had not yet laced her first boot when a crunch of pea-shucks told her that someone else had awakened.

Pa stirred the hearth embers and added goat dung. The orange light brightened, pushing his huge shadow against the wall.

"Is it morning?" Marda leaned up on one arm and squinted at the firelight.

"Just for me," said their father.

He looked to where Miri stood, frozen, one foot in a boot, her hands on the laces.

"No," was all he said.

"Pa." Miri stuffed her other foot in its boot and went to him, laces trailing on the dirt floor. She kept her voice casual, as though the idea had just occurred to her. "I thought that with the accidents and bad weather lately, you could use my help, just until the traders come."

Pa did not say no again, but she could see by the concentrated way he pulled on his boots that he meant it. From outside wafted one of the chanting songs the workers sang as they walked to the quarry. *I hear a work song say winter is long.* The sound came closer, and with it an insistence that it was time join in, hurry, hurry, before the workers passed by, before snow encased the mountain inside winter. The sound made Miri's heart feel squeezed between two stones. It was a unifying song and one that she was not invited to join.

Embarrassed to have shown she wanted to go, Miri shrugged and said, "Oh well." She grabbed the last onion from a barrel, cut off a slice of brown goat cheese, and handed the food to her father as he opened the door.

"Thank you, my flower. If the traders come today, make me proud." He kissed the top of her head and was singing with the others before he reached them.

Her throat burned. She would make him proud.

Marda helped Miri do the inside chores—sweeping the hearth and banking the coals, laying the fresh goat dung out to dry, adding more water to the salt pork soaking for dinner. As Marda sang, Miri chattered about nothing, never mentioning their pa's refusal to let her work. But gloom hung heavy on her like wet clothes, and she wanted to laugh and shake it off.

"Last week I was passing by Bena's house," said Miri, "and her ancient grandfather was sitting outside. I was watching him, amazed that he didn't seem bothered by a fly that was buzzing around his face, when, *smack*. He squashed it right against his mouth."

Marda cringed.

"But Marda, he left it there," said Miri. "This dead fly stuck just under his nose. And when he saw me, he said, 'Good evening, miss,' and the fly . . ." Miri's stomach cramped from trying to keep speaking through a laugh. "The fly wobbled when he moved his mouth . . . and . . . and just then its little crushed wing lifted straight up, as if it were waving hello to me, too!"

Marda always said she could not resist Miri's low, throaty laugh and defied the mountain itself not to rumble as well. But Miri liked her sister's laugh better than a belly full of soup. At the sound, her heart felt lighter.

They chased the goats out of the house and milked the nannies in the tight chill of morning. It was cold on top of their mountain in anticipation of winter, but the air was loosened by a breeze coming up from a valley. The sky changed from pink to yellow to blue with the rising sun, but Miri's attention kept shifting to the west and the road from the lowlands.

"I've decided to trade with Enrik again," said Miri, "and I'm set on wrestling something extra out of him. Wouldn't that be a feat?"

Marda smiled, humming. Miri recognized the tune as one the quarry workers sang when dragging stones out of the pit. Singing helped them to tug in rhythm.

"Maybe extra barley or salt fish," said Miri.

"Or honey," said Marda.

"Even better." Her mouth watered at the thought of hot sweet cakes, honeyed nuts for a holiday, and a bit saved to drizzle on biscuits some bleak winter evening.

At her pa's request, Miri had taken charge of trading for the past three years. This year, she was determined to get that stingy lowlander trader to give up more than he had intended. She imagined the quiet smile on Pa's face when she told him what she had done.

"I can't help wondering," said Marda, holding the head of a particularly grumpy goat while Miri did the milking, "after you left, how long did the fly remain?"

At noon, Marda left to help in the quarry. Miri never spoke about this daily moment when Marda went and Miri stayed behind. She would never tell how small and ugly she felt. *Let them all believe I don't care,* thought Miri. *Because I don't care. I don't.*

When Miri was eight years old, all the other children her age had started to work in the quarry—carrying water, fetching tools, and performing other basic tasks. When she had asked her Pa why she could not, he had taken her in his arms, kissed the top of her head, and rocked her with such love, she knew she would leap across the mountaintops if he asked it. Then in his mild, low voice, he had said, "You are never to set foot in the quarry, my flower."

She had not asked him why again. Miri had been tiny from birth and at age fourteen was smaller than girls years younger. There was a saying in the village that when something was thought to be useless it was "skinnier than a lowlander's arm." Whenever Miri heard it she wanted to dig a hole in the rocks and crawl deep and out of sight.

"Useless," she said with a laugh. It still stung, but she liked to pretend, even to herself, that she did not care.

Miri led the goats up a slope behind their house to the only patches of grass still long. By winter, the village goats worked the hilltop grasses down to stubble. In the village itself, no green things grew. Rock debris was strewn and stacked and piled deeper than Miri could dig, and scree littered the slopes that touched the village lanes. It was the cost of living beside a quarry. Miri heard the lowlander traders complain, but she was accustomed to heaps of rock chippings underfoot, fine white dust in the air, and mallets beating out the sound of the mountain's heartbeat.

Linder. It was the mountain's only crop, her village's one means of livelihood. Over centuries, whenever one quarry ran out of linder, the villagers dug a new one, moving the village of Mount Eskel into the old quarry. Each of the mountain's quarries had produced slight variations on the brilliant white stone. They had mined linder marbled with pale veins of pink, blue, green, and now silver.

Miri tethered the goats to a twisted tree, sat on the shorn grass, and plucked one of the tiny pink flowers that bloomed out of cracks in the rocks. A miri flower.

The linder of the current quarry had been uncovered the day she was born, and her father had wanted to name her after the stone.

"This bed of linder is the most beautiful yet," he had told her mother, "pure white with streaks of silver."

But in the story that Miri had pulled out of her pa many times, her mother had refused. "I don't want a daughter named after a stone," she had said, choosing instead to name her Miri after the flower that conquered rock and climbed to face the sun.

Pa had said that despite pain and weakness after giving birth, her mother would not let go of her tiny baby. A week later, her mother had died. Though Miri had no memory of it save what she created in her imagination, she thought of that week when she was held by her mother as the most precious thing she owned, and she kept the idea of it tight to her heart.

Miri twirled the flower between her fingers, and the thin petals snapped off and dropped into the breeze. Folk wisdom said she could make a wish if all the petals fell in one twirl.

What could she wish for?

She looked to the east, where the yellow green slopes and flat places of Mount Eskel climbed into the gray blue peak. To the north, a chain of mountains bounded away into forever—purple, blue, then gray.

She could not see the horizon to the south, where somewhere an ocean unfolded, mysterious. To the west was the trader road that led to the pass and eventually to the lowlands and the rest of the kingdom. She could not imagine life in the lowlands any more than she could visualize an ocean.

Below her, the quarry was a jangle of odd rectangular shapes, blocks half-exposed, men and women working with wedges and mallets to free chunks from the mountain, levers to lift them out, and chisels to square them straight. Even from her hilltop, Miri could hear the chanting songs in the rhythms of the mallet, chisel, and lever, the sounds overlapping, the vibrations stirring the ground where she sat.

A tingle in her mind and a sense of Doter, one of the quarrywomen, came with the faint command *Lighten the blow.* Quarry-speech. Miri leaned forward at the feel of it, wanting to hear more.

The workers used this way of talking without speaking aloud so they could be heard despite the clay plugs they wore in their ears and the deafening blows of mallets. The voice of quarry-speech worked only in the quarry itself, but Miri could sometimes sense the echoes when she sat nearby. She did not understand how it worked exactly but had heard a quarry worker say that all their pounding and singing stored up rhythm in the mountain. Then, when they needed to speak to another person, the mountain used the rhythm to carry the message for them. Just now, Doter must have been telling another quarrier to lighten his strike on a wedge.

How wonderful it would be, Miri thought, to sing in time, to call out in quarry-speech to a friend working on another ledge. To share in the work.

The miri stem began to go limp in her fingers. What could she wish for? To be as tall as a tree, to have arms like her pa, to have an ear to hear the linder ripe for the harvest and the power to pull it loose. But wishing for impossible things seemed an insult to the miri flower and a slight against the god who made it. For amusement she filled herself with impossible wishes—her ma alive again, boots no rock shard could poke through, honey instead of snow. To somehow be as useful to the village as her own pa.

A frantic bleating pulled her attention to the base of her slope. A boy of fifteen pursued a loose goat through the knee-deep stream. He was tall and lean, with a head of tawny curls and limbs still brown from the summer sun. Peder. Normally she would shout hello, but over the past year a strange feeling had come inching into Miri, and now she was more likely to hide from him than flick pebbles at his backside.

She had begun to notice things about him lately, like the pale hair on his tanned arm and the line between his brows that deepened when he was perplexed. She liked those things.

It made Miri wonder if he noticed her, too.

She looked from the bald head of the miri flower down to Peder's straw-colored hair and wanted something that she was afraid to speak.

"I wish . . . ," she whispered. Did she dare?

"I wish that Peder and I—"

A horn blast echoed so suddenly against the cliffs that Miri dropped the flower stem. The village did not have a horn, so that meant lowlanders. She hated to respond to the lowlander's trumpet like an animal to a whistle, but curiosity overcame her pride. She grabbed the tethers and wrestled the goats down the slope.

"Miri!" Peder jogged up beside her, pulling his goats after him. She hoped her face was not smudged with dirt.

"Hello, Peder. Why aren't you in the quarry?" In most families, care of the goats and rabbits was performed only by those too young or too old to work in the quarry.

"My sister wanted to learn wedge work and my grandmother was feeling sore in the bones, so my ma asked me to take a turn with the goats. Do you know what the trumpeting is about?"

"Traders, I guess. But why the fanfare?"

"You know lowlanders," said Peder. "They're so *important*."

"Maybe one had some gas, and they trumpeted so the whole world would know the good news."

He smiled in his way, with the right side of his

mouth pulling higher than the left. Their goats were bleating at one another like little children arguing.

"Oh, really, is that so?" Miri asked the lead goat as if she understood their talk.

"What?" said Peder.

"Your nanny there said that stream was so cold it scared her milk right up into her mutton chops."

Peder laughed, stirring in her a desire to say something more, something clever and wonderful, but the wanting startled all her thoughts away, so she clamped her mouth shut before she said something stupid.

They stopped at Miri's house to tie up the goats. Peder tried to help by taking all the tethers, but the goats started to butt one another, the leads tangled, and suddenly Peder's ankles were bound.

"Wait . . . stop," he said, and fell flat to the ground.

Miri stepped in to try to help and soon found herself sprawled beside him, laughing. "We're cooked in a goat stew. There's no saving us now."

When they were finally untangled and standing upright, Miri had an impulse to lean forward and kiss his cheek. The urge shocked her, and she stood there, dumb and embarrassed.

"That was a mess," he said.

"Yes." Miri looked down, brushing the dirt and gravel from her clothes. She decided she had better tease him quickly in case he had read her thoughts. "If there's one thing you're good at, Peder Doterson, it's making a mess."

"That's what my ma always says, and everyone knows she's never wrong."

Miri realized that the quarry was silent and the only pounding she heard was her own heartbeat in her ears. She hoped Peder could not hear it. Another trumpet blare roused them to urgency, and they set off running.

The trader wagons were lined up in the village center, waiting for business to begin, but all eyes were on a painted blue carriage that rolled into their midst. Miri had heard of carriages but never seen one before. Someone important must have come with the traders.

"Peder, let's watch from—" Miri started to say, but just then Bena and Liana shouted Peder's name and waved him over. Bena was as tall as Peder, with hair browner than Miri's that hit her waist when loose, and Liana with her large eyes was acknowledged the prettiest girl in the village. They were two years older than Peder, but lately he was the boy they most preferred to smile at.

"Let's watch with them," said Peder, waving, his smile suddenly shy.

Miri shrugged. "Go ahead." She ran the other way,

weaving through the crowd of waiting quarry workers to find Marda, and did not look back.

"Who do you think it could be?" asked Marda, stepping closer to Miri as soon as she approached. Even in a large group, Marda felt anxious standing alone.

"I don't know," said Esa, "but my ma says a surprise from a lowlander is a snake in a box."

Esa was slender, though not as small as Miri, and shared the same tawny hair with her brother, Peder. She was eyeing the wagon, her face scrunched suspiciously. Marda nodded. Doter, Esa and Peder's mother, was known for her wise sayings.

"A surprise," said Frid. She had shoulder-length black hair and an expression of near constant wonderment. Though only sixteen, she was nearly as broad-shouldered and thick-armed as any of her six big brothers. "Who could it be? Some rich trader?"

One of the traders looked their way with a patronizing smile. "Clearly, it's a messenger from the king."

"The king?" Miri felt herself gawk like a coarse mountain girl, but she could not help it. No one from the king had been to the mountain in her lifetime.

"They're probably here to declare Mount Eskel the new capital of Danland," said the trader.

"The royal palace will fit nicely in the quarry," said

the second trader.

"Really?" Frid asked, and both traders snickered. Miri glared at them but did not speak up, afraid of sounding ignorant herself.

Another trumpet blared, and a brightly dressed man stood on the driver's bench and yelled in a high, strained voice, "I call your ears to hearken the chief delegate of Danland."

A delicate man with a short, pointed beard emerged from the carriage, squinting in the sunlight that reflected off the white walls of the old quarry. As he took in the sight of the crowd, his squint became a pronounced frown.

"Lords and ladies of . . ." He stopped and laughed, sharing some private joke with himself. "People of Mount Eskel. As your territory has no delegate at court to report to you, His Majesty the king sent me to deliver you this news." A breeze tapped his hat's long yellow feather against his brow. He pushed it away. Some of the younger village boys laughed.

"This past summer, the priests of the creator god took council on the birthday of the prince. They read the omens and divined the home of his future bride. All the signs indicated Mount Eskel."

The chief delegate paused, seemingly waiting for a response, though what kind Miri had no notion. A cheer? A boo? He sighed, and his voice went higher.

"Are you so remote that you don't know the customs of your own people?"

Miri wished that she could shout out just the right answer, but like her neighbors, she was silent.

A few traders chuckled.

"This has long been a Danlander custom," said the chief delegate, pushing the wind-beaten feather away from his face. "After days of fasting and supplication, the priests perform a rite to divine which city or town is the home of the future princess. Then the prince meets all the noble daughters of that place and chooses his bride. You may be certain that the pronouncement of Mount Eskel shocked many Danlanders, but who are we to argue with the priests of the creator god?"

From the tightness of his tone, Miri guessed that he had indeed tried to argue with the priests of the creator god and failed.

"As is the tradition, the king commanded an academy be created for the purpose of preparing the potential young ladies. Though law dictates the academy be formed in the chosen town, your village does not"—he squinted and looked around—"indeed, does not have any buildings of appropriate size for such an undertaking. Given these circumstances, the priests agreed the academy could be lodged in the old stone minister's house near the mountain pass. The king's servants are even now preparing it for use." The wind tapped the feather on his cheek. He swatted it like a bee.

"On the morrow, all the girls in this village aged twelve to seventeen are ordered to the academy to prepare themselves to meet the prince. One year from now the prince will ascend the mountain and attend the academy's ball. He himself will select his bride from among the girls of the academy. So let you prepare."

The updraft thrust the feather into his eye. He tore it from his hat and threw it at the ground, but the wind snatched it up and sent it flying out from the village, over the cliff, and away. The chief delegate was back in his carriage before the feather was out of sight.

"Snake in a box," said Miri.

Chapter Two

Water in the porridge
And more salt in the gruel
Doesn't make a belly
Full, not a bellyful

"Let's do what we came for," shouted a trader.

His voice was an invitation to break the silence. Even such strange news could not delay the most important trading of the year.

"Enrik!" Miri jogged to the trader she had dealt with for the past two years. He was lank and pale, and the way he looked down his thin nose at her reminded Miri of a bird that had gone too long without a grub.

Enrik drove his wagon to the stack of finished stones that represented her family's portion of the past three months' work. Miri pointed out the unusually large size of one block and the quality of the silver grain in others, all the while eyeing the contents of his wagon and calculating how much food her family would need to get through the winter.

"These stones are easily worth your haul," said Miri, trying her best to mimic Doter's warm, solid tone of voice. No one ever argued with Esa and Peder's ma. "But to be nice, I'll trade our stones for everything in your wagon except one barrel of wheat, one bag of lentils, and a crate of salt fish, so long as you include that pot of honey."

Enrik clicked his tongue. "Little Miri, your village is lucky any traders come all this way just for stone. I'll give you half of what you asked."

"Half? You're joking."

"Look around," he said. "Haven't you noticed fewer wagons this year? Other traders hauled supplies to the academy instead of to your village. Besides, your pa won't need so much with you and your sister gone."

Miri folded her arms. "This academy business is just a trick to cheat us, isn't it? I knew it had to be something sneaky because no lowlander is going to make a girl from Mount Eskel into royalty."

"After the news of the academy, no family with eligible girls is going to barter for any better, so you'd best take my offer before I drive away."

Sounds of frustrated conversations blew around the town center. Peder's ma was red-faced and yelling, and Frid's ma looked ready to hit someone.

"But I . . . I wanted . . ." She had visualized coming

home triumphant with a load fit to feed two families.

"But I wanted . . . ," Enrik mimicked her in a squeaky voice. "Now don't let your chin get to quivering. I'll give you the honey, just because someday you might be my queen."

That made him laugh. As long as she got to bring home some honey, Miri did not mind his laugh. Not much, anyway.

Enrik drove to her house and helped her unload, at least. It gave Miri a chance to take some pleasure in how often he stumbled and tripped on the stony turf.

Miri's house was built of rubble rock, the plain gray stone the quarriers pulled out of the earth to uncover linder. The back of her house leaned against the sheer wall of a dead quarry, the one of her father's childhood that had offered linder with soft blue streaks. Linder and rubble rock debris piled as high as the windowsills.

Miri busied herself around the house all afternoon, sorting and storing their winter supplies, shying away from the thought that it would not be enough to see the three of them through winter. They could eat many of the rabbits and perhaps kill a goat, but that loss would make things even tighter the next winter and the next. *Stupid, cheating lowlanders.*

When the sunlight streaking through her shutters was orange and hazy, the sound of pounding began to falter. By the time her pa and Marda opened the door, it was night. Miri had ready pork, oat, and onion stew, with fresh cabbage to celebrate a trading day.

"Evening, Miri," said her pa, kissing the top of her head.

"I got Enrik to give us a pot of honey," said Miri.

Marda and Pa hummed over her small triumph, but the poor trading and strange news of the academy were on their minds, and no one was able to pretend cheeriness, even over honey.

"I'm not going," said Miri as she prodded her chilling stew. "Are you, Marda?"

Marda shrugged.

"They think the village could do without half the girls?" said Miri. "Who'd help you in the quarry with Marda gone? And without me, who would do all the housework and tend the rabbits and the goats and all the things that I do?" She bit half her lip and looked at the fire. "What do you think, Pa?"

Her father rubbed a callused finger over the rough grain of the table. Miri held still as a rabbit listening.

"I'd miss my girls," he said.

Miri exhaled. He was on their side, and he would not let the lowlanders take her away from home. Even so, she found it difficult to finish dinner. She hummed to herself a song about tomorrows.

Chapter Three

Tomorrow's a red flush in the western sky
Tomorrow's a black hush in the middle night
Tomorrow swears the truth of now, now, and now
In the trembling blue gasp of the morning light

Before dawn, Miri woke to trumpeting. The same sound that in the day had been curious and even comical was now unsettling. Before she could stand, her pa was at the door, and what he saw made him frown.

Miri's first thought was bandits, but why would they attack Mount Eskel? Every villager knew the story of the last bandit attack, before Miri was born, when the exhausted outlaws had finally reached the village at the top of the mountain only to find little worth stealing and a horde of men and women made strong by years in the quarry. The bandits had run off with empty hands and a few more bruises and had never returned.

"What is it, Pa?" asked Miri.

"Soldiers."

Miri stood behind him and peered under his lifted arm. She could see pairs of torch-bearing soldiers all over the village. Two approached their door, their faces visible by torchlight—one was older than her pa, tall, with a hard face, and the other seemed but a boy dressed up.

"We've come to collect your girls," said the older soldier. He checked a thin wood board burned with marks that Miri did not understand. "Marda and Miri."

Marda was standing on the other side of their pa now. He put his arms around both their shoulders.

The soldier squinted at Miri. "How old are you, girl?"

"Fourteen," she said, glaring.

"Are you certain? You look—"

"I'm fourteen."

The young soldier smirked at his companion. "Must be the thin mountain air."

"And what about you?" The older soldier turned his doubtful gaze to Marda.

"I'll be eighteen in the third month."

He smacked his lips together. "Just missed it, then. The prince will be eighteen in the fifth month of this year, and no girl older than the prince is allowed. We'll just be taking Miri."

The soldiers shifted their feet in the rock debris. Miri looked up at her pa.

"No," Pa said at last.

The younger soldier snorted and looked at his companion.

"I thought you were joking when you said they might resist. 'No,' he says, as though it's his choice." He leaned forward and laughed.

Miri laughed back loudly in the young soldier's face, surprising him into silence. She could not stand to have a lowlander mock her pa.

"What a good joke, a boy pretending to be a soldier," said Miri. "But isn't it awfully early for you to be away from your ma?"

He glared. "I'm seventeen and—"

"Are you really? That muggy lowlander air does stunt a thing, doesn't it?"

The young soldier started forward as if he would strike Miri, but her pa stepped in front of her, and the older soldier knocked back his companion and whispered angrily into his ear. Miri had enjoyed returning the insult, but now she felt cold and tired. She leaned closer to her pa and hoped she would not cry.

"Sir," said the older soldier courteously, "we are here to escort the girls safely to the academy. These are the king's orders. We mean no harm, but I do have instructions to take any resisters directly to the capital."

Miri stared, wishing the soldier would take it back. "Pa, I don't want you arrested," she whispered.

"Laren!" one of the village men, Os, called out to their father. "Come on, we're meeting."

The soldiers followed them to the village center. While the adults and soldiers conversed, Miri and Marda stood in a huddle of other village girls and boys, watching and waiting for a decision. The adults argued with the soldiers, who in turn tried to calm everyone and make assurances that their girls would be safe, well cared for, and as near as a three-hour walk.

"But how will we manage without the girls to help in the quarry?" asked Frid's ma.

Of course no one asked, "How will we manage without Miri?" She folded her skinny arms and looked away.

They argued about needing the girls, the shorter food supply that winter, the threat of arrest, and the unknown future the girls would meet at the academy. The soldiers continued to answer questions and claim that attending the academy was an honor, not a punishment. Miri saw Os ask her father a question, and after a thoughtful pause, her father nodded agreement. Miri felt chills.

"Girls, come on over," Os shouted.

The girls stepped away from the boys and made their way to the gathering of adults. Miri noticed that Marda stayed behind.

"Girls." Os looked them over and rubbed his beard with the back of his hand. Though he was large and was known for his temper, there was a softness in his eyes. "We've all agreed that the best thing is for you to attend the lowlander academy." Sighs and moans rippled through the crowd. "Now don't worry. I believe these soldiers that all will be well with you. We want you to study hard and do your best and be respectful when you should. Go gather your things and don't drag your feet. Show these lowlanders the strength of Mount Eskel."

Suddenly Peder was beside her. "Are you going?" he asked.

"Yes, I guess. I don't know." She shook her head, trying to rattle her thoughts straight. "Are you? I mean, of course you're not—you're a boy. I meant to ask, do you wish I weren't? Never mind."

His mouth twisted into a mischievous smile. "You want me to say that I'll miss you."

"I'll miss you. Who else can make a mess of everything?"

Walking away, Miri wished she could undo her words and instead say something nice, something sincere. She had turned to go back when she saw that he was talking with Bena and Liana.

Marda returned from their house with a bundle of clothes and a bag of food for Miri, and Pa pulled them both into his arms. Miri sank into his chest, his body blocking the light of torches and the sound of good-byes. Surely his embrace meant that he loved her, though he did not say it. Surely he would miss her. But Miri could not help wondering how he would react if Marda, the daughter who worked by his side, were going to the academy. Would he have protested more? Would he have refused then?

Say that you'd miss me too much, she thought. *Make me stay.*

He only hugged her tight.

Miri felt torn in half, like an old shirt made into rags. How could she bear to leave her family and walk into some lowlander unknown? And how could she bear to admit that her pa did not care if she stayed?

Her father's arms relaxed, and she pulled away. The noise of gravel underfoot said that most of the girls were already on the road.

"I guess I should get on," she said.

Marda gave her a last hug. Pa only nodded. Miri took her time walking away in case he called out for her to come back.

Just before leaving the village, Miri paused to look back. Four dozen houses leaned against the stripped walls of a dead quarry. At the edge of the village stood the stone chapel, its ancient wood door carved with the story of the creator god first speaking to people. The sky was rust and yellow in the east, illuminating the village as though by firelight.

She could see the hilltop where she spent afternoons with the goats and surprised herself by feeling a tiny flash of relief that she would not sit there today, watching the quarriers work below. The crunching noise of the girls on the march beckoned her with a promise of something different, a place to go, a chance to move forward.

"Hurry on," said a soldier bringing up the rear, and Miri complied.

The girls had drifted into small groups as they walked, and Miri was unsure which to join. For the past few years, all her childhood friends had begun to work in the quarry, and Miri had grown used to solitude in her house and on the hilltop with the goats. Around others, Marda was usually by her side.

Ahead walked Esa and Frid, and Miri jogged to catch up. Though Esa had no use of her left arm since a childhood accident, she still worked in the quarry when need was great, and Frid performed even the most difficult quarry tasks. Miri thought they were marvelous. If they thought Miri a burden on the rest of the village, as she had often feared, then she would never let them see she cared.

Despite her uncertainty, Miri took Esa's hand. Village girls always held hands while walking. Doter, Esa's mother, had once said it was an old custom meant to keep them from slipping off cliffs, though Miri had felt as safe as a goat scampering alone around Mount Eskel since she was five.

"Do you have any idea what all this is really about?" Miri asked.

Esa and Frid shook their heads. She eyed them, trying to read in their expressions if they wished she would go away.

"I'd wager this princess nonsense is a trick thought up by the traders," said Miri.

"My ma wouldn't let me leave if she thought I'd come to harm," said Esa. "But she doesn't know what to make of it either."

Frid was staring straight ahead as though looking at death itself. "How would a prince decide who to marry, anyway? Would they have a contest for the princess like we do on a holiday, lifting or running or throwing stones for distance?"

Miri laughed, realizing too late from Frid's serious expression that she had not meant it as a joke. Miri cleared her throat. "I don't know, but I have a hard time believing lowlanders marry for love, anyway."

"Do lowlanders love anything?" said Frid.

"Their own smells, I imagine," said Miri.

"At least there will be one less stomach to fill in my house," said Esa, glancing back as if thinking about home. Her voice softened. "Look, there's Britta. I can't believe she's going, too."

"She's a lowlander," said Frid.

"But she's been on the mountain all summer, so I guess she means to stay," said Esa.

Miri glanced over her shoulder at Britta, walking alone between two groups. The lowlander girl was fifteen and delicate, as though she had never wrangled a goat or pounded out a wheel of cheese. Her cheeks were ruddy like the sun side of an apple, and the feature gave her a merry, pretty look when she flashed a rare smile.

"I've never spoken to her," said Miri.

"She's never spoken to most people," said Esa. "Doesn't she ignore everyone who talks to her?"

"She did in the quarry," said Frid. "She carried water this summer, but when workers asked for a drink, she acted as if she were deaf. After a couple of weeks, Os said, what's the use? And sent her home."

The story had circulated that when her lowlander parents had died in an accident, her only living relations had turned out to be distant cousins from Mount Eskel. So one spring morning Britta had come riding on a trader wagon with a bag of clothes and food supplies bought from the sale of her parents' remaining possessions. At least now she was wearing a shirt and leggings like the rest of them instead of dresses cut from dyed cloth.

"I can't believe Peder thinks she's pretty," said Esa.

Miri coughed. "He does? I don't think she is. I mean, she acts like she's too good to talk to anyone."

"All lowlanders think they're above us," said Frid.

"We're the ones on the mountain," said Miri, "so aren't we the ones above *them*?"

Esa smirked at one of the soldiers, and Frid made fists. Miri smiled, warmed by their shared sentiments.

For three hours they wove around the puddles, holes, and boulders of quarries long ago abandoned, until at last they spied the roof of the academy. Miri had seen it six years ago, when the village had held their spring holiday inside its stone walls. Afterward they had deemed the walk too long to do so again.

It was called the stone minister's house, and the villagers assumed that the structure had once housed a court minister who oversaw the quarry. No such person now lived on the mountain, but the house did prick in Miri a desire to see what other wonders there might be in the lowlander kingdom, just out of her sight.

Even from afar Miri could detect a white gleam—polished linder had been laid as the foundation, the only finished linder she had ever seen. And though the rest of the house had been built from gray rubble rock, the stones were squared, smoothed, and fitted together in perfection. Three stairs led to the main door and columns supporting a carved pediment. Workers perched on the roof, fixing weather damage. Other lowlanders replaced empty windows with glass panes, pulled up grass growing between the floorstones and steps, and swept away years of dirt.

The arriving girls milled around, peeking into wagons or gawking at the commotion. There were twenty of them, from Gerti who was barely twelve to Bena who was seventeen and a half.

A woman appeared in the building entrance. She was tall and lean, her cheeks sunken, her hair flat on the end like a chisel. She waited, and Miri felt self-conscious of the mountain girls, all standing about and staring, unsure of what to do.

"Step closer," said the woman.

Miri tried to line up even with the others, but no one else seemed to have her idea, and they formed a small mob rather than a straight line.

"I see I did not underestimate the degree of finishing mountain girls would require." The woman pressed her lips in a twitch. "I am Olana Mansdaughter. You will address me as Tutor Olana. I've heard about Danland's outlying territories—no towns, no marketplace, no noble families. Well. Once you pass these columns and enter this building, you're agreeing to obey me in all things. I must have absolute order in this academy if ever I am to turn uneducated girls into ladies. Is that understood?"

Frid squinted at Olana. "So, are you saying that we don't have to go to the academy if we don't want to?"

Olana clicked her tongue. "This is even worse than I expected. I may as well set up the academy in a barn."

Frid's expression became troubled, and she looked around, trying to fathom what she had done wrong.

"Please excuse our rudeness, Tutor Olana." Katar stepped forward. Her curly hair was reddish like the clay beds beside the village stream. She was the tallest girl after Bena, and she held herself as though she were taller than any man and twice as tough.

"We must seem pretty rustic to you," said Katar, "but we're ready to enter the academy, learn the rules, and do our best."

Some of the girls seemed none too eager, with backward glances and shifting feet, but Os had been clear. Most nodded or murmured in agreement.

Olana seemed doubtful but said, "Then let's have no more nonsense and in you go."

As soon as Olana was beyond earshot, Katar turned to glare at the girls. "And try not to act so ignorant," she hissed.

Miri stared down as she entered the building, letting the tip of her boot slide across a floorstone—white as cream, with the palest streaks of rose. It seemed remarkable that with no one to tend it, the stone had held its luster for so many decades. The villagers had to clean and oil the wooden chapel doors regularly to keep them undamaged.

Olana led the girls through the cavernous house, warning them to stay silent. The walls and floor were bare, and Olana's voice and the click of her boot heels echoed over Miri's head and under her feet, making her feel surrounded.

"The building is too large for our needs," said Olana, indicating that most of the dozen or more chambers would be left closed and unused so they would not need to be heated through the winter. The academy would confine itself to three main rooms.

They followed Olana into a long room that would serve as a bedchamber. Several rows of pallets lay on the floor. The far wall held one hearth for warmth and one window facing home. Miri mused that the girls on pallets farthest from the fire would be mighty cold.

"I have a separate bedchamber just down the corridor, and if I hear noises at night, I . . ." Olana paused, an expression of disgust crawling over her face. "What a stench! Do you people live with goats?"

They did, of course, live with goats. No one had the time to build a separate house for the goats, and having them indoors helped both the goats and the people keep warm in the winter. *Do I really stink?* Miri looked away and prayed no one would answer.

"Well, a few days here might air out the odor. One can hope."

Next they visited the huge chamber in the center of the building that would serve as a dining hall. A large hearth with a carved linder headpiece was the only indication that the room might have been grand once. Now it was bare but for simple wood tables and benches.

"This is Knut, the academy's all-work man," said Olana.

A man stepped through the adjacent kitchen

doorway and cast his gaze up and down as though unsure if he should meet their eyes. His hair was gray around his temples and in his beard, and he gripped a stirring spoon in his right hand in a way that reminded Miri of her pa with his mallet.

"He will be very busy," said Olana, "as will you all, so don't waste time addressing him."

The introduction seemed brusque to Miri, so she smiled at Knut as they left, and he returned a flicker of a smile.

Olana led the girls back through the main corridor and into a large room with three glass windows and two hearths. Wood fires were a rare luxury in the village, and the smoke was fresh and inviting. Six rows of chairs with wooden boards secured to their arms filled up most of the space. At the head of the room, a shelf of leather-bound books hung over a table and chair.

Olana directed them to sit in rows according to their age. Miri took her seat on a row with Esa and the two other fourteen-year-olds, put her hands in her lap, and tried to appear attentive.

"I will begin with the rules," said Olana. "There will be absolutely no talking out of turn. If you have a question, you will keep it to yourself until I ask for questions. Any nonsense, any mischief, any disobedience, will result in punishment.

"This teaching position was supposed to be an honor. I'll have you know I left a post at the royal palace tutoring the prince's own cousins to climb up here and baby-sit dusty goat girls, though I suppose you don't even know what the royal palace is."

Miri sat up straighter. She knew what the palace was—a very big house with a lot of rooms where the king lived.

"Well, deserved or not, you are now part of a historic undertaking. In the past two centuries, the princess academy has merely been a formality, with the noble girls of the chosen town gathering for a few days of society before the prince's ball.

"Since Mount Eskel is merely a territory, not a province, of Danland, and you cannot boast of any noble families, the chief delegate believes the academy must be taken very seriously this generation. Never before have the priests named a territory the chosen region. I may tell you that the king and his ministers are quite uneasy about marrying the prince to an unpolished girl from an outlying territory. Therefore the king granted me the solemn responsibility to verify that every girl sent to the ball is fit to become the princess. If any of you fail to learn the basic lessons I teach you this year, you will not attend, you will not meet the prince, and you will return to your village disgraced.

"Now, I understand that there is a true Danlander among us, is that so?" Olana sighed at the silence that followed. "I'm requesting a response. If any of you were not born on this mountain, you have my permission to speak now."

Most of the girls had turned to look at Britta sitting in the fifteen-year-olds' row before she raised her hand.

"I was born in the city of Lonway, Tutor Olana."

Olana smiled. "Yes, you do have a look in you of some breeding. Your name?"

"Britta."

"Is that it? What's your father name? I would expect the villagers to be ignorant of such a formality, but not one from Lonway."

Miri adjusted in her seat. They were not ignorant—a girl took her father's name and a boy took his mother's name to help distinguish them from anyone else with the same first name. Mount Eskel shared some Danlandian traditions, it seemed.

"I'm orphaned this year, Tutor Olana," said Britta.

"Well then," said Olana, looking ill at ease at how to respond. "Well, such things happen. I'll expect you to lead the class in your studies, of course."

The stares pointed at Britta began to turn to glares.

"Yes, Tutor Olana." Britta kept her eyes on her hands. Miri suspected that she was gloating.

Then began the instruction. Olana held up a shallow box filled with smooth yellow clay. With a short stick called a stylus, she marked three lines in the clay.

"Do any of you know what this is?"

Miri frowned. She knew it was a letter, that it had something to do with reading, but she did not know what it meant. Her embarrassment was appeased somewhat by the general silence that followed.

"Britta," said Olana, "tell the class what this is."

Miri waited for her to spout the brilliant answer and revel in her knowledge, but Britta hesitated, then shook her head.

"Surely you know, Britta, so say so now before I lose patience."

"I'm sorry, Tutor Olana, but I don't know."

Olana frowned. "Well. Britta will not be an example to the class after all. I am curious to see who will jump forward to take her place."

Katar sat up straighter.

While Olana explained the basics of reading, Miri's thoughts kept flitting to Britta. One summer trading day, Miri had overheard Britta read words burned into the lid of a barrel. Was she pretending ignorance now so she could amaze Olana later with how quickly she would seem to learn? *Lowlanders are as clever as they are mean*, thought Miri.

Her attention snapped away from Britta when Gerti, the youngest girl, raised her hand and interrupted Olana's lecture. "I don't understand."

"What was that?" said Olana.

Gerti swallowed, realizing that she had just broken the rule of speaking out of turn. She looked around the room as if for help.

"What was that?" Olana repeated, pulling her vowels long.

"I said, I just, I'm sorry . . . I'm sorry."

"What is your name?"

"Gerti," she breathed.

"Stand up, Gerti."

Gerti left her chair slowly, as though longing to return to its safety.

"This little girl is giving me an opportunity to illustrate the consequences of rule breaking. Even the prince's cousins are punished when they choose to misbehave, though I think I'll employ slightly different methods for you. Follow me, Gerti."

The tutor led Gerti out of the room. The rest of the girls sat motionless until Olana returned with two soldiers.

"Gerti is in a closet thinking about speaking out

of turn. These fine soldiers will be staying with us this winter. Should any of you have ideas about questioning my authority, they are here to make it clear. Each week that you show a marked improvement, you are permitted to return home for the rest day, so let us continue our studies with no further interruptions."

At sundown, the workmen on the roof stopped hammering and Miri first noticed the noise for its absence. Pa and Marda would be home by now, white dust wafting from their work clothes. Marda would say how she missed Miri, her conversation, maybe even her cabbage soup. What would Pa say?

In the dining hall, the girls ate fried herring stuffed with barley porridge, onions, and unfamiliar flavors. Miri suspected it was a fancy meal and meant to mark a special occasion, but the strange spices made it feel foreign and unkind, a reminder that they had been taken away from home.

No one spoke, and the sounds of sipping and chewing echoed on bare stone walls. Olana dined in her own room, but no one could be certain if she was listening and would emerge at the first sound, trailing soldiers in her wake.

Later in their bedchamber, the tension had wound so tight, it burst into a flurry of whispered conversations.

Gerti reported on the closet and scratching sounds she had heard in the dark. Two of the younger girls cried for wanting to go home.

"I don't think it's fair the way Olana treats us," Miri whispered to Esa and Frid.

"My ma would have a thing to say to her," said Esa.

"Maybe we should go home," said Miri. "If our parents knew, they might change their minds about making us stay."

"Hush up that kind of talk, Miri," said Katar. "If Olana overheard, she'd have the soldiers whip us all."

The conversation lagged and then stopped, but Miri was too tired and anxious to sleep. She watched the night shadows shift and creep across the ceiling and listened to the low, rough breathing of the other girls. Her pulse clicked in her jaw, and she held on to that noise, tried to take comfort from it, as if the quarry and home were as near as her heart.

Chapter Four

Tell my family to go ahead and eat
To make it home I'd have to move my feet
But the mount's made stone where my feet numbered two
And I've swallowed more dust than I can chew

The next day, the workers finished the repairs and left the academy, leaving Olana, Knut, two soldiers, and an unfamiliar silence. Miri missed the pounding and scraping and beating, sounds that meant work in the quarry was going on as usual and no one was injured. The quiet haunted her all week.

In the mornings before lessons started, the girls spent an hour doing chores, washing and sweeping, fetching wood and water, and helping Knut in the kitchen. Miri spied the other girls stealing minutes of conversation at the woodpile or behind the academy. Perhaps they did not mean to exclude her, she thought, perhaps they were simply used to one another from working together in the quarry. She found herself wishing desperately for Marda at her side, or Peder, who had somehow remained her friend, unchanged, over the years.

She glanced at Britta carrying a bucket of water to the kitchen and wondered for the first time if there was more to her silence than just pride. Then again, she was a lowlander.

Near the week's end, the girls could barely follow their lessons, so rich was the anticipation of being able to sleep by their home fires and attend chapel, to see their families and report all they had suffered and learned.

"We can walk home tonight," Esa whispered to Frid when Olana left the room for a moment. Then she turned to Miri, her expression full of happy anticipation. "I don't care how late, so we'll have all day tomorrow!"

Miri nodded, pleased to have been included.

When Olana continued the reading instruction, Miri noticed Gerti rubbing her forehead as if thinking gave her pain. No doubt the time she had spent in the closet their first day put her behind. She would need extra help if she was ever to catch up.

There was a village saying that Miri thought of more than any other: "The unfair thing stings like nettles on bare skin." It was not fair that Olana had let Gerti lag behind and did nothing about it. Miri's instinct prodded her to do something, so she went to Gerti and crouched by her desk, clinging to a wild hope that Olana would see the justice in her action and let her be.

"I'll help you, Gerti," said Miri quietly. She drew the first character on Gerti's tablet. "Do you know what this is?"

"What is going on?" asked Olana.

"Gerti missed the first lesson," said Miri. "She needs help."

"Come here, both of you," said Olana.

Gerti's mouth dropped open, and she gripped the sides of her desk.

"Gerti didn't do anything," said Miri, standing.

She wished for words to defend herself, but Olana did not ask for an explanation. She picked up a whittled stick as long as her arm.

"Hold out your hand, Miri, palm up."

Miri stuck out her hand and was dismayed to see it tremble. Olana lifted the stick.

"Wait," said Miri, pulling her hand back. "I was helping. How can you hit me for helping?"

"You were speaking out of turn," said Olana. "Continuing to do so won't excuse you."

"This isn't fair," said Miri.

"On the first day in class, I made clear that a

broken rule would result in a punishment. If I don't follow through on my word, that would be unfair. Hold out your hand."

Miri could think of no response. She opened her fingers to expose her palm. Olana brought the stick down with a crack and a sting, and Miri's arm shook with the effort of not pulling away. A second time, and a third. She looked at the ceiling and tried to pretend she had not felt a thing.

"And now, miss, we should deal with you," said Olana, turning to the younger girl.

"Gerti didn't ask for help." Miri swallowed and tried to calm her quavering voice. "It was my fault."

"So it was. Now you all have learned that those who speak out of turn choose punishment for themselves and anyone they speak to."

"So if I speak to you, Tutor Olana, will you get the lashes?"

Miri had hoped to draw out a laugh and ease the friction, but the girls stayed as quiet as hunted prey. Olana's lips twitched in anger.

"That will earn you three lashes on your left hand as well."

Gerti took her three lashes and Miri hers again on the other hand. When the lesson continued, Miri found it difficult to grip her stylus. She kept her head down and focused on making each character just right in the clay. Sometimes she could hear Gerti's breath catch in her throat.

"Olana." A soldier entered the room. "Someone from the village has come."

Olana followed him out, and Miri could hear her voice echo from the corridor. "What do you want?"

"The village sent me to ask when the girls are coming home," came the voice of a boy.

Expectation crossed Esa's face, and Bena and Liana whispered and giggled. Miri's own insides felt buoyant and sick at once. Peder was just outside.

"You tell the village that everything is fine. I know the soldiers explained to their parents that I must have absolute freedom to teach and train the girls if I am to succeed. They will visit home when they earn it, and disrupting my class with questions will not bring them home any sooner."

Olana came back and resumed her lecture. Through the window, Miri could see Peder standing in front of the academy, trying to see past the sun's glare on the windows. He kicked the ground, picked up a piece of scrap linder larger than his fist, and ran back toward the village.

At noon when Olana dismissed them to the dining

hall, Miri's palms were still red. Her thoughts and emotions played a game of tug-rope inside her. That she should be punished for helping Gerti. That she should be ignored and humiliated. That Peder had come all this way and been dismissed, and she had not been able even to wave. And added to it the ever-present shame of being useless.

"This is stupid," Miri said as soon as they had exited the classroom.

Katar, who walked beside her, said, "Hush," and glanced back to see if Olana had heard.

"Let's go home," Miri said a little louder. Her gut still felt hollow since seeing Peder, and her stinging hands felt bigger than her caution. "We can leave before the soldiers even know we're gone, and if we all run at once, they'll never catch us."

"Stop!" The commanding voice made Miri halt midstep. No one turned around. The click of Olana's boot heels came closer.

"Was that Miri speaking?"

Miri did not answer. She thought if she spoke, she might cry. Then Katar nodded.

"Well," said Olana, "another offense. I did say earlier that speaking out was punishable not only to the perpetrator, but to her listeners, isn't that right?"

Some of the girls nodded. Katar glared.

"None of you will be returning to your families tomorrow," said Olana. "You will spend the rest day in personal study."

Miri felt as if she had been slapped. A cry of protest arose.

"Silence!" Olana raised her walking stick. "There is nothing to debate. It's time you learned you are part of a country with laws and rules, and there are consequences for disobedience. Now back to the classroom. There will be no noon meal today."

The girls made more noise than usual taking their seats, as if to give voice to their anger, scraping the wood chair legs against the stone floor, clattering their tablets on their desks. In the quiet that followed, Miri heard Frid's stomach moan in hunger. Normally, Miri would have laughed. She pressed her stylus so hard into the clay that it snapped in two.

That afternoon, Olana let the girls go out for some exercise. They pulled on cloaks and hats, but once outside Miri took hers off. The instant cold felt fresh and freeing after all day in the fire-heated classroom. She longed to run like a rabbit, so light that she would leave no tracks to follow.

Then she noticed that she was standing alone and the others were in a group, facing her. The oldest girls stood in front, arms crossed. Miri thought she understood how a lost goat would feel on meeting a pack of wolves.

"It's not my fault," said Miri, afraid admitting that she was sorry would condone Olana's actions. "Her rules are unfair."

Frid and Esa glanced back to see if Olana was near, but it was understood that outside, the girls could talk.

"Don't rush to apologize," said Katar, flipping her orange hair out of the neck of her cloak.

Miri's chin began to quiver, and she covered it with her hand and tried to act unaffected. If everyone thought her too weak to work in the quarry, at least she could show them she was too strong to cry.

"I was trying to stand up for all of us. This is another case of lowlanders treating mountain folk like worn-through boots."

Bena glared. "You were warned, Miri. Why can't you just follow the rules?"

"No one should have to follow unfair rules. We could all run home right now. We don't have to stay and put up with closets and palm lashings and insults. Our parents should know what's going on." Miri wished that she could find the right words to express her anger and fear and longing, but to her own ears her argument sounded forced.

"Don't you dare," Katar said, folding her arms. "You

do that and they might shut down the academy and ask the priests to announce some other place as the home of the future princess. Then we'll all lose our chance because of you, Miri."

Miri stared. No one was laughing. "You really think they'll let one of us be a princess?" she asked, her voice dry and quiet.

"Of course, acting the way Miri does she'd never be chosen, but there's no reason the rest of us can't try." Katar's usually confident voice began to sound pinched and strained, as if, for some reason Miri could not guess, she was desperate to convince the others. "Being a princess would mean more than just marrying a prince—you'll see the rest of the kingdom, live in a palace, fill your belly every meal, have a roaring fire all winter long. And you'll do important things, the kinds of things that affect an entire kingdom."

Be special, important, comfortable, happy. That was what Katar was offering with her plea to stay. Some of the girls shuffled closer, leaned slightly toward Katar, as if feeling the pull of her story. Miri was embarrassed to feel chills sneak across her own skin. What would her pa think of her if she was chosen out of all the other girls to be a princess?

It was a lovely idea, a beautiful story, and for a moment she wished she could believe it, but she knew no lowlander would let a crown sit on a mountain girl's head.

"It won't happen . . . ," Miri whispered.

"Oh, be quiet," said Katar. "You've made us lose a meal and a return home. Don't you dare spoil our chances of becoming a princess."

Olana called, and all the girls, even Gerti, turned their backs on Miri and went inside. Miri stared at the ground, hoping no one would see how her face burned. She followed them in at the back of the line.

Britta walked just ahead of her in the corridor. Before they entered the classroom, the lowlander girl turned and smiled. Miri almost smiled back before she realized that Britta must be glorying in her disgrace. She frowned and looked away.

The next day was unbearable. Although Olana insisted returning to the village each rest day should be an occasional privilege, she also declared she must have a break from the girls unless she were to go mad. So the girls passed that day unsupervised in the classroom. Miri sat alone, aware that even as the noise of levity grew, she was not invited to take part. When a conversation fell on the topic of Olana, Miri offered what she thought was a remarkable imitation of the tutor's pinched lips. No one laughed, and Miri resigned herself to practicing her letters in silence.

She spent the next week counting hours until rest

day. Surely after all the girls could sleep by their own fires for a night, the tension would ease. Perhaps when Miri told her pa about the rules and the palm lashing, he would admit he had made a mistake, that he needed her home just as much as he needed Marda. Just three more days to freedom, then two, one.

Then that night, snow fell.

The school awoke to white drifts that rivaled the village's strewn rock debris for covering everything and threatening to keep piling up to their windowsills. The girls were quiet as they looked outside, imagining the distance back to the village, the hidden holes and boulders they would not be able to see for the snowfall, weighing the danger against their desire to go home.

"To the classroom, then," said Olana, ushering them away from their bedchamber window. "No one will be walking through this weather, and if the tale I hear of this mountain is correct, we'll be huddling inside until spring thaw."

Olana stood at the head of the class, her hands clasped behind her back. Miri felt herself sit up taller under that gaze.

"Katar has informed me that some doubt the legitimacy of this academy. I won't risk having flabby-minded girls to present to His Highness next year, so let me assure you, the prince will choose one of you to marry, and you will live in the palace, be called 'princess,' and wear a crown."

Olana called to Knut, and he entered the classroom with something silvery in his arms. Olana took it from him and shook it out. It was a gown, and perhaps the most beautiful thing Miri had ever seen besides her mountain view. The cloth was unlike anything she knew, sleek and light, and reminded her of a running stream. It was gray in its folds and shimmered silver where the window light touched it. Pale pink ribbons gathered the fabric at the shoulders and waist, and tiny rosebuds scattered on the long full skirts.

"This dress," said Olana, "is like the ones that a princess would wear. A royal seamstress crafted it for whichever girl finishes this year as head of the academy."

The girls gasped and sighed and oohed to one another, and for once Olana did not hush them.

"Let us see who wants this gift the most. The victorious girl will be introduced to the prince as the academy princess, and she will wear this dress and dance the first dance. His bride will still be his to choose, but the academy princess is sure to make a significant impression."

As Olana spoke, her eyes flicked to Frid, and Miri

imagined she was hoping that the broad girl would not be the victor, as she was too big for the dress as it was. But Frid's face did not reveal any concern for the garment's size. She ogled the silvery thing with eyes even wider than usual. Miri tried her best to look unimpressed but could not help wondering, *What would it feel like to wear such a dress?*

"Be warned that you will not easily meet my expectations," said Olana. "I have very real doubts that mountain girls are capable of measuring up to other Danlanders. Your brains are naturally smaller, I've heard. Perhaps due to the thin mountain air?"

Miri glowered. Even if Olana's promises were true, Miri would not want to marry a lowlander, a person who despised her and the mountain. Prince or no, he would be like Olana, like Enrik and the traders, like the chief delegate frowning at the sight of the mountain folk and all too eager to get back into his carriage and drive away.

She rubbed her eyes, and the clay on her fingers got under her lids and made them sting. She was tired of lowlanders belittling her and tired of wondering if they were right. She was going to show Olana that she was as smart as any Danlander. She was going to be academy princess.

Chapter Five

Everybody knows that the best things come last
That's why my ma says I'm last in everything
I always wear cast-off shirts and worn-through boots,
Scrape the bottom of the pot, and bathe downstream

Once, words had been invisible to Miri, as unknown and uninteresting as the movements of a spider inside a rock wall. Now they appeared all around her, standing up, demanding notice—on the spines of books in the classroom, marking the barrels of food in the kitchen and storeroom, carved into a linder foundation stone: *In the thirteenth year of the reign of King Jorgan.*

One day Olana threw out a parchment, and Miri snatched it from the garbage pile, kept it under her pallet, and practiced reading it by firelight to the sound of snores. It listed the names of the academy girls and their ages. Miri felt a thrill tickle her heart to read her own name in ink. "Marda Larendaughter" was there as well, though her name was crossed out. On the list, Britta had no father name.

Throwing herself into learning helped Miri ignore the painful chill of solitude around her. As they fell two, three, and then four weeks into winter, Miri felt utterly frozen in her blunder. She thought about trying again to make amends, but the silence of the other girls meant they had not forgotten how Miri had cost them the last possible visit home before snow fell. Even Esa did not save Miri a place in the dining hall; even Frid failed to offer a casual smile. Miri shrugged away the hurt and told herself they had never truly been her friends.

Miri missed Peder. She missed the ease of always knowing exactly what he was trying to say, and she missed the agitation of his nearness when her fingers felt thick and clumsy and her mouth dry. Watching him swing a mallet or throw a stone, listening to the pleasant rasp of his voice, the way he laughed whenever he heard her laugh. Feeling herself lean to him as she would to warm herself at a fire.

Outside the classroom window, the snow kept falling. Miri looked away, struck by the throbbing in her chest. She had caught herself longing for spring and their return and was sliced by sharp truth—she missed Marda, Pa, and Peder, but did they miss her? She focused on her tablet and studied twice as hard.

One late afternoon, Olana set the girls loose outside. They had spent all day at their desks except for two outhouse breaks and one of Knut's increasingly sad meals—salt fish boiled to mush and potatoes without so much as a ribbon of grease or grain of salt to cheer them. Frid had received a palm lashing for falling asleep during quiet study, and Gerti had spent an hour in the closet for whimpering when she could not draw the last letter of the alphabet.

Miri watched the girls file out and considered joining them. She yearned to forget that she had cost them a journey home and go out smiling and laughing, or even just to run through the snow alone and relish the cold air stinging her cheeks.

But if she stayed indoors, she would have the classroom to herself. She had been hoping for this chance all week.

When she heard the last footsteps fade down the corridor, Miri stood and stretched. Thirteen books stood on a high shelf above Olana's desk. Miri had counted them, had read their spines and anticipated what might be inside. She stood on her toes and pulled one down.

The words *History of Danland* were painted in white

on the dark leather spine. The book smelled dusty and old but also carried a sweet tang, a hint of something inviting. She opened to the first page and started to read, pronouncing the words in a reverent whisper.

She did not understand a thing.

Three times she read the first sentence, and though she could speak the individual words, she could not understand what they all meant together. She shut the book and opened another, *Danlander Commerce*. What was Commerce, anyway? She put it away and opened another, and another, and felt an urge to start throwing them. She had just pulled down a thinner book titled simply *Tales* when the sound of boot heels on flagstones made her heart jump. Miri did not know if she would be punished for borrowing a book, and it was too late to put it back. She stuffed it under her shirt.

"Miri," said Olana, entering. "Not even a stretch today? Do the other girls hate you so much?"

Olana's comment stung. Miri had not known her distance from the others was obvious. She pressed the hidden book to her side and sauntered out of the classroom.

For the next two weeks, when the others went outside, Miri curled up in a corner of the bedchamber, the book of tales on her lap. She struggled at first, but soon the words made sense together, and then the sentences built on the page, and then the pages made stories. It was marvelous. Stories were inside those tedious letters they had been learning all along, stories like the ones she heard at spring holiday or that Peder's grandfather told before a fire on a cold night. And now she could read them by herself.

Several days later, Olana took a book from the shelf and handed it to some of the older girls. Though Katar read better than the rest, she still stumbled over the unfamiliar words, sounding them out laboriously. Britta as well could barely get through a sentence. Her ruddy cheeks turned even redder. Miri considered that she had been mistaken and Britta had never been able to read.

"What a shame." Olana took the book from Britta and turned to Miri. "Well, you're a young one, but you seem focused of late."

The book was *History of Danland*, the dark brown tome Miri had tried and failed to read before. Olana opened it to the second page and pointed to a paragraph. Miri's tongue felt made of clay. She cleared her throat, gripped the book, and began.

"Our ancestors came from the north and farmed the fertile central plains. They also raised herds of cattle, horses, mountain goats, sheep, and fowl. Along the coast, fishing became one of their most important industries, as it is today."

The words seemed to glide across Miri's tongue, each one falling into place. She had never seen the passage before, but studying the book of tales had made reading anything easier. She stuttered over a couple of words but sounded them out all right.

"Well, girls," said Olana when Miri finished, "if the prince were coming tomorrow, you know who would wear the silver gown."

Miri felt a grin break her face and had the unlikely impulse to give Olana a hug. Katar's frown deepened into a glare. Miri swallowed and tried to look modest, but it was too late. Katar was usually the best in the class, and surely she thought Miri's smile meant that she was gloating. Her victory soured like milk left standing.

That evening as she returned from the outhouse, Miri halted at the sound of hushed voices coming from the front of the academy. She took a few steps backward, easing her boots through the hard shell of the snow. Whispering meant secrets, and it raised a shiver of curiosity on Miri's skin. She leaned against the wall and strained to pick words out of the quiet drone. Her own name spoken in a whisper made her feel queasy.

". . . can't stand Miri . . . acts like she's so smart . . ." That voice belonged to Bena. ". . . never liked the way she hung on Peder . . . becoming unbearable . . ."

". . . just lucky today," said Liana. "She won't . . ."

"She's just fourteen," said Katar, speaking much louder than the others. "What are you worried about?"

Bena mumbled something else. Katar snickered.

"There's no chance of that. One of the older girls will win."

"I get the idea, Katar, that you think you should be princess," said Bena, her voice scaling higher. "But as long as . . ." She returned to whispering, and Miri could hear no more.

Miri started on her way again, and the girls quieted as she passed. Liana smiled uncomfortably, Bena glared at the ground, but Katar stared at Miri, her expression unrepentant. Miri returned that stare as though it were a challenge. She had just raised a defiant eyebrow when she tripped on one of the front steps and fell flat in the snow. She jumped to her feet and ran inside, chased by the sound of the older girls chuckling.

That night, she lay on her pallet inhaling the darkness. It was a comfort to her to be awake as the others slept, as though she elected to be alone, as if she enjoyed it. The bedchamber fire was not high enough to warm her on her pallet at the far end of the room, and she shivered and wished for something to hope for. She closed her eyes and saw the folds of the silver dress twist and shimmer beneath her lids. Her dreams of becoming academy princess wrapped around her and eased the chill.

Chapter Six

Whiskers taut, front teeth bared
Shaking breath, round eyes scared

Winter kept falling from the sky, building up under the windowsills, and crawling with frost over the panes. When clouds kept the sun from burning the frost away, Miri could see the outside world only as a grayish blur. So much time indoors, so much time with no one to talk to, was making her feel wretched. Her body ached, her skin itched as though she were wrapped tight in wool and could not stretch.

The next time Olana dismissed the girls outside, Esa turned to Miri before leaving the classroom and gestured that she should follow. Miri sighed with anticipation. If Esa forgave her, perhaps the others would as well. Her determination to be just fine alone melted under the bright hope of making everything all right.

She had one small task first. After waiting until all the girls left the classroom, Miri crept to the bookshelf for a chance to return the volume of tales. She was standing on her tiptoes, inching the book back into place, when a sound at the door startled her. She jumped and dropped the book.

"What are you doing?" asked Olana.

"Sorry," said Miri, picking up the fallen book and dusting it off. "I was just . . ."

"Just dropping my books on the floor? You weren't planning on stealing one, were you? Of course you were. I would have allowed you to borrow a book, Miri, but I won't tolerate stealing. In the closet with you."

"The closet?" said Miri. "But I wasn't . . ."

"Go," said Olana, herding Miri like a sulky goat.

Miri knew the place, though she had never been in it. She looked back before stepping inside.

"For how long?"

Olana shut the door on Miri and clicked the lock.

The sudden lack of light was terrifying. Miri had never been any place so dark. In winter Marda, Pa, and Miri slept by the kitchen fire, and in summer they slept under the stars. She lay on the floor and peered under the door into the thin band of gray light. All she could see were the bulges of floorstones. Faint shouts and happy screeches drifted in from the girls playing in the snow. Esa would think Miri had ignored the invitation, that she did not care to be her friend. Miri inhaled sharply, then coughed on the dust.

A sound of scurrying brought her upright. She heard it again, a noise like fingernails tickling a smooth surface. Miri held herself tight to the wall. Again. Some small animal must be in the dark with her. It might be just a mouse, but not knowing made the thing strange and unnerving. She tried to see past the shadows. Her eyes adjusted, bringing some definition to the darker shapes, but there was not enough light.

When the scurrying stopped, Miri stayed standing until her back ached and her head felt heavy. She was tired of staring at the dark, imagining she saw faces staring back or tiny forms darting in the corners. Boredom made her sleepy. At last she lay down, resting her head on her arms, and watched the slit under the door for a sign of Olana coming to free her. The cold of the stones soaked through her wool shirt and raised bumps on her skin, making her shiver and sigh at once. She fell asleep without resting.

Miri woke to a tug and a horrible feeling. Was someone in the room trying to wake her? The light bleeding through the door was even dimmer, and the throbbing in her body told her it was hours later.

She felt it again, a tugging on her scalp. Something was caught in her braid. She wanted to scream, but terror clamped down on her breath. Every spot of her skin ached with the dread of what might be touching her. It felt strong, too big to be a mouse.

The tip of a tail licked her cheek. A rat.

Miri sobbed breathlessly, remembering the rat bite that had killed a village baby some years before. She did not dare to call out for fear of spooking the beast. The tugging stopped, and Miri waited. *Is it free? Is it gone?*

Then the thing thrashed harder. Close to her ear Miri heard a dry squeal.

She could not move, she could not speak. How long would she have to lie there until someone came for her? Her thoughts lunged and rolled, seeking some way out, some comfort.

"'Plumb line is swinging, spring hawk is winging, Eskel is singing.'" She whispered as quietly as a slow-moving stream. It was a song of celebration, of springtime, using a weighted cord to square a stone, looking up to a hawk gliding, feeling that the work was good and the whole world just right. As she sang, she tapped a linder floorstone with the pads of her fingers, as though she were working in the quarry and using quarry-speech to a friend nearby.

"Mount Eskel is singing," she whispered, and began to change the words, "but Miri is crying. A rat she is fighting." She almost made herself laugh, but the sound of another snarl tore it from her throat. Afraid now even to whisper, she sang in her head, still tapping her fingers in time and with her silent song pleading with the darkness for someone to remember her.

The door opened, and candlelight pierced her eyes.

"A rat!" Olana had her walking stick in hand and used it to prod at Miri's hair.

"Hurry, hurry," Miri said, shutting her eyes.

She heard a squeal, a scamper, and she jumped to her feet and embraced Olana. She was trembling too hard to stay upright on her own.

"Yes, all right, that's enough," said Olana, prying Miri's arms from around her.

The cold and her fright made Miri feel half-dead. She hugged herself against a chill that threatened to shake her like a wind-stirred seedpod.

"I've been locked up for hours," she said, her voice croaking. "You forgot about me."

"I suppose I did," said Olana without apology, though deeper lines in her brow spoke that she was disturbed by the sight of the rat. "It's well that Gerti remembered you, or I might not have come until morning. Now get on to bed."

Miri now saw Gerti, her eyes as wide as a mink's as she stared at the gaping darkness of the closet. Olana took her candle and left them in shadows, so Miri and Gerti hurried back to their bedchamber.

"That was a rat," said Gerti, sounding haunted.

"Yes." Miri was still trembling as though she were frozen cold. "Thanks for remembering me, Gerti. My heart would've stopped if I'd been in there another moment."

"It was strange how I thought of you, actually," said Gerti. "When we came back from break this afternoon, you were just gone. Olana never said anything, and I was afraid to ask. Then when we were getting ready for bed, I had this horrible memory of when I was locked up, and I'd heard scratching noises in there, and I was so sure you were locked up in the closet, and I . . . I don't know, but I knew there was a rat. It was almost like . . . Oh, never mind."

"Like what?"

"I'm sure I guessed you were in the closet because, where else would you be? And I thought I heard a rat when I was in there, too, so that's how I knew. But the way my vision kind of shivered when I thought about it, the way the idea of you and the rat was so clear, it reminded me of quarry-speech."

Miri felt new chills. "Quarry-speech? But—"

"I know that's silly. It couldn't have been quarry-speech, because we're not in the quarry. I'm just glad we didn't get into trouble. When I went to Tutor Olana's bedchamber and begged her to come get you, she threatened all kinds of punishment."

Miri did not say anything else. New possibilities were painting themselves before her in the dark.

Chapter Seven

I've a lever for a bandit
And a chisel for a rat
I've a mallet for a she-wolf
And a hammer for a cat

One afternoon two or three years earlier, Miri and Peder had sat on a grazing hill above the village. They were young enough that Miri had not yet begun to worry that her nails were dirty and broken or that Peder was bored with her words. He was then working six days a week in the quarry, and Miri had pressed him for details.

"It's not like building a fire or tanning a goat hide, Miri, not like any other chore. When I'm working, it's as though I'm listening to the stone. Don't scowl at me. I can't explain it any better than that."

"Try."

Peder had squinted at the linder shard in his fingers. He was using a small knife to carve it into the shape of a goat. "When everything's going right, it feels like the songs we sing on holidays, the men taking one part, the women another. You know how the harmony sounds? That's how working linder feels. It may seem silly, but I imagine that linder is always singing, and when I get my wedge in just the right crack and bring down my mallet just so, I feel like I'm singing back. The quarry songs the workers sing aloud are to keep time. The real singing happens inside."

"Inside how?" Miri had asked. She was plaiting miri stems to keep from appearing too interested. "How does it sound?"

"It doesn't actually sound like anything. You don't hear quarry-speech with your ears. When something is wrong, it feels wrong, like when I know the person next to me is pushing too hard with his lever and could crack the stone. When that happens, and it's too noisy in the quarry to just say, 'Ease up on that lever,' I tell them in quarry-speech. I don't know why it is called quarry-speech since it is more like singing than speaking, only you're singing *inside*. And it sounds louder, if you can describe it like that, when someone's speaking directly to you, but everyone nearby can hear."

"So, you just sing somehow and other people can hear it," she had said, not understanding.

Peder had shrugged. "I'm talking to a person, but I'm singing, but not out loud. . . . I don't know how to describe it, Miri. It's like trying to explain how to run or swallow. Stop pestering me or I'll go find Jans and Almond and we'll play a boys-only game."

"You do and it'll be the last game you ever play."

Peder had not understood why it was important to Miri to understand quarry work, so she had not pressed anymore. She liked that he did not guess her frustration and isolation, that he assumed she remained the same carefree Miri she had always been.

Miri now let the memory of this conversation roll around in her mind, adding to it everything she thought she knew about quarry-speech. It had always been part of the quarry and so something she could not do. *Had Gerti heard quarry-speech?* she wondered. *Can it work outside the quarry after all?* Just the possibility was as enticing as the smell of honey cakes baking next door.

The day after the rat, Miri was doing morning chores, sweeping the academy corridors. She waited until no one else was near, then ducked into a cold, unused room and tried to quarry-speak. She rapped the broom handle on a flagstone, trying to mimic a quarry tool, and sang a work song aloud. Then she changed the song to carry the message she wanted to speak. "I've a lever for a bandit and a chisel for a rat. The rat was in the closet till the tutor made it scat."

She knew from watching the quarry that the workers

sang and tapped when they spoke quarry-speech, but just changing the words to the song did not feel right.

The real singing happens inside, Peder had said.

"Maybe in the same way that singing is different from speaking," she whispered, trying to reason it out, "quarry-speech is different from just thinking."

With a song, the words flowed together in a manner that was different from normal conversation. There was a rhythm to it, and the sounds of the words fit together as though they were made to be sung side by side. *How can I do that same thing with my thoughts?* she wondered.

Miri spent the rest of the chore hour trying it out. She made up songs as she often did, not only singing aloud, but focusing on the sound of her song, trying to make her thoughts resonate and flow in a different way, and focusing on the tiny tremors her knuckles sent through the linder stone. Did the speech rush into the ground? She closed her eyes and imagined she was singing her thoughts right down into the stone, singing of the rat and her desperate need that night in the closet, pushing her internal song with a quavering desire to be heard.

For the briefest moment, she felt a change. The world seemed to shudder, and her thoughts clicked together. She gasped, but the feeling was gone as quickly as it had come.

Olana rapped her stick in the corridor to announce the end of chores, and Miri swept up her pile of dirt and ran to the classroom. She watched Gerti take her seat, trying to detect any sign that the younger girl had heard. Miri risked a quick question before Olana entered.

"How are you feeling, Gerti?"

"Fine." Gerti sat down, scratched her neck, and then, with a glance at the door to make sure the tutor was not near, she whispered, "I guess I can't get that rat out of my mind. I was just remembering again when I was in the closet. . . ."

Olana came in and Gerti whipped herself back around. Miri rubbed the chills from her arms. She believed it had worked, but questions still kept her brow wrinkled. Of all the girls, why had Gerti heard her quarry-speech that night? And why again?

When the girls fled the classroom at the next break, Katar fetched a book from the shelf and sat in her chair with a loud thud.

"Don't look so shocked, Miri," said Katar without raising her eyes from the book. "You're not the only one who can study during breaks. I guess you think academy princess is yours, no competition."

"No," said Miri, wishing for a good, biting response to pop into her head. All she could think of was, "But maybe you do."

Katar smiled, apparently thinking that retort too weak to deserve a response. Miri agreed silently. She could force herself to stay in the classroom for only a couple of minutes before slinking away.

Over the next several days, Katar's presence in the classroom during breaks kept Miri scurrying other places to test her quarry-speech—in a corner of the bedchamber, behind the outhouse, and once in the closet, though just stepping inside made her skin itch as if covered in spiders. More and more often, when she rapped the ground and sang a quarry song, a curious sensation followed. Everything before her seemed to vibrate like a flicked tree branch, and a sharp, warm feeling flared behind her eyes. The idea of the rat and the closet felt round and real, as though she were living the moment again. She felt her song throb inside her and imagined it going down into the stone, into the mountain, down and then up again to find someone who could hear.

But often, nothing happened at all. And she could not figure out why.

Quarry-speech is supposed to be for talking to other people, she thought. *Maybe I need to try it with someone.*

Miri did not dare approach any of the girls who worked in the quarry. Would they think she was foolish to try? Would they laugh? One morning while

Britta read aloud in class, Miri watched her, thinking that Britta did not know enough about quarry matters to laugh at her and was not likely to tattle to the other girls. Miri was reluctant to try it with a lowlander, but her anticipation of discovery was making her impatient.

The next afternoon break, Miri joined the others outside. The sun's glare off the snow made her eyes water, but it seemed the most beautiful day Miri could remember. The sky was achingly blue. The snow that crunched under her boot spread over stone and hillock like spilled cream. The cold made the world feel clean and new, a day for beginnings.

Miri walked straight past the group of older girls and greeted Britta. "Hello."

Britta had been standing alone and seemed startled to be addressed.

"Want to go for a walk?" said Miri, hoping to get Britta alone.

"All right."

As they walked away, Miri reached to take Britta's hand. Britta flinched as if surprised at the touch.

"It's normal to hold hands while walking, you know," said Miri, guessing from Britta's reaction that common hand-holding was a mountain custom.

"Oh, sorry," said Britta. "So everyone holds hands?

Boys and girls and everyone?"

Miri laughed. "Girls and boys hold hands when they're little." She could not remember when she and Peder had last held hands. As they grew up, the casual touch of wrestling and playing had just stopped. "If a girl and boy hold hands when they're older, it *means* something."

"I see." Britta took Miri's hand.

They trudged through untouched snow around the side of the building, and Miri glanced back to see if anyone else was near. Just a little farther.

"I wanted to tell you, I'm sorry Olana put you in the closet," said Britta.

Miri nodded, her eyes wide. "So am I. There was a rat in there, and I don't mean Olana. An actual rat tried to nest in my hair." She shivered. "I found a whisker in my braid the next morning, and I think I might have squealed aloud."

Britta smiled. "You did."

"Well, I'm glad my horror was amusing to someone," said Miri, making sure to add a good-natured grin so Britta would know that she was teasing.

"Olana shouldn't put people in closets or strike us," said Britta, negotiating the deeper swells of snow. "I think she's too quick to punish."

Miri pressed her lips together in a surprised frown.

If Britta disapproved, then perhaps Olana's attitude was not typical of lowlanders. Or perhaps Britta was not a typical lowlander herself.

"I didn't think they'd be so mean," said Britta. "Since one of us will be the princess."

"Do you think one of us really will be?"

"I don't think they would lie." Britta puffed a visible breath. "But lately I feel as stupid as a tree stump, so I don't dare believe my own thoughts."

They sat on the linder steps that led to the academy's back entrance, and Miri thought she could chance it now. She tapped a rhythm, thought of a quarry song, even hummed aloud. She was trying to quarry-speak the *Take care* warning she had often heard echoing out of the quarry. For just a moment, everything appeared to quake and she felt that resonance, but Britta did not flinch.

Miri nearly groaned aloud. She had been certain those sensations were a sign of quarry-speech, but if it had worked, Britta would have reacted in some way to the warning.

Unless . . . She looked Britta over. *Unless lowlanders are deaf to it.*

The more she let this idea soak in, the likelier it seemed. Quarry-speech was just for quarriers, just for the mountain. That made Miri smile to herself while she sang. Something mountain folk could do that low-landers could not. Something even Miri could do. A talent. A secret.

"Should I . . . Do you want me to sing with you?" asked Britta.

Miri stopped. "Oh no. I was, you know, humming for fun."

"You don't have to stop," said Britta. "It sounded nice. I just didn't know what you expected, because I seem to be always doing the wrong thing. Lately. Sorry to interrupt. Keep going."

"We should be heading back anyway."

"All right."

The girls turned to retrace their steps. Miri teetered when her foot hit a deep patch of snow and she let go of Britta's hand, but Britta grabbed her arm and helped steady her.

"Thanks," said Miri.

"Thank you. I mean . . ." Britta looked up, struggling for words. "Thanks for talking to me." She pressed her lips together as though she were afraid to say any more.

"Sure," Miri said casually, though inside she was reeling. The girl had thanked her just for talking.

As they came back around to the front of the building, Liana whispered something to Bena, and

Bena smirked. Miri hung on to Britta's arm even tighter, determined not to be cowed by their looks.

When Olana called them back in, Knut was standing at the head of the classroom cradling a rectangular package wrapped in a coarse brown cloth.

"Your progress has been sluggish of late," said Olana. She smoothed her chisel-sharp hair behind her shoulder. "Perhaps it's due to the winter and the separation from your families, or perhaps you're simply not taking this endeavor seriously. I thought it was time for a reminder of why you're here."

Olana removed the cloth and held up a colorful painting much more detailed than the chapel's carved doors. It illustrated a house with a carved wood door, six glass windows facing front, and a garden of tall trees and bushes bursting with red and yellow flowers.

"This house stands in Asland, the capital, not a long carriage ride from the palace." Olana paused as if anticipating a dramatic reaction. "It will be given to the family of the girl chosen as princess."

Several voices gasped, and Miri could not be certain if hers had been one. Perhaps all of this was real after all. There was proof. Pa and Marda could live in that beautiful house and never dress in cloth too threadbare to keep off the sun or half starve in the winter. She longed to give them something so precious and perfect. What would her pa think of her then?

But to get that house for her family, Miri would have to be the princess. She closed her eyes. The idea of marrying a lowlander still confused and frightened her. And what of Peder? No. She crushed that thought, not daring to hope that he could ever see her as anything but little Miri, his childhood friend.

She looked again at the painting. Before the academy, her only wish had been to work in the quarry alongside her pa. Now other possibilities were beginning to nudge and prod her.

What of the lowlands?

What of being a princess?

That night, Miri was still awake hours into the dark when she heard the distant crash of rockfalls. The quarry workers said a rockfall was the mountain strengthening itself against the attacks of the previous day. Her pa said her ma had thought it was the mountain itself shouting a midnight hello.

All her life, Miri had been awakened by such a noise. It almost always came at night, as though the mountain knew the quarry was empty and the shifting rocks would not crush anyone in their fall. It comforted Miri to hear the crash and moan and remember that she was still on her mountain. She was not ready to give up on the mountain completely, not ready to give up on her pa.

Seeing the painting had let her believe that she *could* leave the mountain, that she might even desire to. The threat of departure made home feel very dear. She wanted to speak back to the mountain, send some greeting in a childish hope that it would hear her and accept her as one of its own.

She splayed her hand on a floorstone and tapped a rhythm with her fingertips. She wished she could shout it out; she wished the mountain really could understand. "She's as lovely as a girl with flowers in her hair," Miri sang in a whisper. "She's as bright as a spring sun drying rain from the air."

It was an ode to Mount Eskel sung at spring holiday, and singing it now wrapped her in memories of the good moments on her mountain. She sang inside, inventing her own song about the tender warmth of a spring breeze, night bonfires, miri chains dangling from her neck, brushing Peder's fingers as she turned in the dance, the heat from the fires that made her feel snuggled against the mountain's chest.

The gray-and-black shadows in the bedchamber shivered, and a sensation entered her as if she had hummed deep in her throat. Quarry-speech. Miri groaned to herself. *Why doesn't it work all the time?* she thought. Another rockfall resounded in the distance, and Miri imagined the mountain was laughing at her. She smiled and nestled deeper into her pallet.

"I'll figure you out," she whispered. "You'll see."

Chapter Eight

My toes are colder than my feet
My feet are colder than my ribs
My ribs are colder than my breath
My breath is colder than my lips
And my lips are purple and blue, purple and blue

Miri woke shivering, and she hopped around as she did her chores, trying to warm her toes. In a mountain winter, the iciness often eased after snow fell, but for the past week the skies had been clear. And a glance out the window told the girls no relief from the cold would come today—clouds heavy with unshed snow slumped onto the mountain, burying everything in wet fog.

Everyone groaned and complained, and Miri knew she should be miserable, too, but instead she felt wrapped up and hidden, a bright secret in a magpie's nest. She stared at the white nothingness outside the classroom window, cozy with her discovery of quarry-speech and anxious to understand it more. She pulled her thoughts back to hear Olana announce that their studies were about to change.

For nearly three months the focus had been on reading, but now Olana introduced other subjects: Danlander History, Commerce, Geography, and Kings and Queens, as well as princess-forming subjects such as Diplomacy, Conversation, and the one that made Miri want to roll her eyes—Poise. Well, she would do it if it meant she could stop Olana's insults and prove that a mountain girl had as many brains as any lowlander.

Her eyes flicked to the painting, and her desires plunged and stumbled inside her. She wanted to give her family that house, yet she did not want to marry a lowlander. She longed to see some of the world they were learning about and find in it a place of her own, yet she was afraid to give up her mountain. No solution she could imagine would make everything just right.

During their lessons on Poise, the girls took off their boots and balanced them on their heads. They walked in circles. They learned how to walk quickly (on toes, toes kept behind the hem of the skirt, fluid, arms slightly bent) and slowly (toe to heel, toe to heel, hands resting on skirt). They learned a deep curtsy for a prince, and as Miri bent her leg and bowed her head, she first believed that she would actually meet a prince. They practiced a shallow curtsy for a peer and understood that they were never to curtsy to a servant.

"Though in truth," said Olana, "as you are not from one of the kingdom's provinces, you would be considered less than a servant in any Danlander city."

To Miri, studying Conversation was as ridiculous as learning Poise. They had all been able to talk since they were toddlers; what more was there to learn? But at least when studying Conversation, the girls were allowed to speak to one another, following the correct principles, of course.

Olana paired the girls and designated their rank. Miri was pleased to be matched up with Britta, even though Olana assigned Miri to be her lesser.

"You must know your rank and that of your interlocutor," said Olana. Miri frowned and looked around. No one dared to interrupt and ask what "interlocutor" meant. "The person of lower rank always defers to the other. This is just for practice, of course, as there are few in the kingdom who would be considered of lower rank than any of you."

Olana's insults were like biting flies stinging her nose, and Miri felt ready to swat her. Britta bumped her with her elbow and smiled, as if guessing her thoughts.

"However, one of you will be elevated in rank next year," said Olana, "so you all must practice against the possibility. Lessers should be certain of the name and rank of their betters. In correct conversation, you will use this often. You may begin."

"All right, Lady Britta," said Miri under the whir of conversation that filled the classroom.

Britta frowned. "You don't need to call me that."

"You're my better," said Miri, "so let's make you a lady, my lady Britta."

"All right, then, Miss Miri."

"Oh, *Lady Britta?*" said Miri with a nasal tone she imagined rich people must use.

"Yes, *Miss Miri?*" Britta mimicked the same affect.

"I do hope all your lords and ladies are fat and happy, Lady Britta."

"All fat, none happy, Miss Miri."

"Indeed, my lady Britta? How lovely for you to go to court with a palace full of plump, bawling lords and ladies rolling down the corridors."

"It is lovely," said Britta with a laugh.

"You're very pretty when you smile, Lady Britta. You should do it more."

Britta smiled softer and ducked her head.

Olana interrupted the practice to croon on about Conversation, the importance of repeating the name and title, asking questions, and always bringing the conversation around to the other person.

"Never offer any information about yourself," said Olana. "Not only for courtesy, but also to protect your secrets, should you have any, which I doubt. For example, suppose you are at a ball and you're feeling very warm. Can anyone tell me how to make this observation to the prince without talking about yourself?"

Katar's hand shot up. Olana called on her.

"It seems to be quite stuffy in here. Are you feeling warm, Your Highness?"

"Nicely done," said Olana.

Miri frowned at Katar and her smug little grin. Olana asked what one could say if the prince asked you how you were feeling. Miri raised her hand as fast as she could.

"Um, I've been eager to meet you, Your Highness. How was your journey?"

Olana raised one brow. "That might be all right, if without the 'um.'"

Katar smirked at Miri.

"Stupid Conversation," Miri said to Britta when they returned to individual conversations. "Learning to read was good, but this stuff is silly. I'd rather be cleaning pots."

Britta shrugged. "I guess it's important, but I don't really like talking about betters and lessers and all. This is just good manners. It seems to me that if you want to make a good impression, you should treat people as your betters, whether Olana thinks they are or not."

"You're not dull in the head after all," said Miri. "Why do you pretend to be?"

Britta gaped, looking both affronted and embarrassed. "I don't pretend anything, and I am . . . I mean, I'm just . . ."

"You could read all along, couldn't you?" Miri whispered.

Britta seemed to consider denying it, then shrugged. "I didn't want to be the only one who could read and let Olana put me up as an example against everyone else. I was having a hard enough time . . . with people up here."

"Britta, I'm sorry, I didn't . . ."

Britta nodded. "I know. I've heard how the traders talk. I see how Olana treats you. Of course you would think all lowlanders are the same. But Miri, I don't think like them. I don't."

The next morning, Olana introduced the rules for diplomatic negotiations, starting with *State the problem* and ending with *Invite mutual acceptance*, then rushed through the long list of general principles of Diplomacy.

"Tell the truth as plainly as possible," Olana read from a book. Her usually loose voice was forced, as if she were embarrassed to be teaching principles she herself did not follow. "Listen carefully to your allies and enemies to know their minds. The best solutions don't come through force. Acknowledge your faults and declare your plan to amend them."

Miri did her best imitation of Olana's twitching lips. Britta smiled behind her hand.

"Now then, let's look briefly at Commerce," said Olana, "just enough to keep you from embarrassing yourselves too horribly in front of the prince."

Once the lesson began, Miri had to consider if mountain folk might actually be duller than lowlanders. She thought Commerce was just a fancy word for how they traded linder for other goods, but Olana blathered about supply and demand, markets, merchants, and commodities. It was as if she made it all sound more complicated than it was just to make the girls feel stupid. At least, Miri hoped that was the case.

At the next break, Miri opened the book on Commerce to see if she could puzzle it out. After five minutes and the beginnings of a frustration headache, she slammed the book closed. Perhaps her head was worn from constantly trying to reason out how quarry-speech worked, or perhaps she just was not smart enough.

Through the window she could see Frid throwing snowballs for distance and Esa laughing at something sixteen-year-old Tonna had said. Even Katar was outside today, sitting on the steps and sunning her face. The snow measured up to Miri's waist in the swells. High winter.

The rabbit coats would be thickest now, and that meant slaughter time. It was a small celebration to have fresh meat for the stew and fur for a new hat or mitts. Miri hated the chore, but she did it every year to spare Marda, who wept to see any creature die. Miri wondered if Marda would steel herself to do the killing this year or if Pa would think to take care of it some evening.

Miri's eyes went to the painting of the house. Wishing to leave her mountain felt like giving up on her pa, and she could not bear to do that. But with that house, she could keep her family close and still travel to new places and learn new things. And if she won, Marda would never have to kill a rabbit and wash off the blood in a snowdrift. Pa would never have to add more water to the gruel to get them through a late-winter dinner. They could sit in the shade of their large house and sip sweet drinks, learn to play lowlander instruments, and stare at the flowers.

Mount Eskel's scattered trees and dull grasses could not stand up to the lowland's gardens. It made Miri wonder if rumors were true that the lowlanders had a gift for making things grow.

Knut entered the classroom and stopped short when he saw Miri. "I thought you were all outside. I just came to clean."

"Hello, Knut," she said. He did not respond or even nod, and that made her laugh. "Are you forbidden to talk out of turn, just like us?"

Knut smiled then, and his short beard stuck out even more. "More or less. But I don't think she'll put me in the closet for saying hello."

"I promise not to tell. Knut, have you ever seen the house in this painting?"

"What, the princess house? No, I don't believe so, though there're plenty of the like down in Asland and the other big cities. Pretty garden that one has. My father was a gardener for such a place most of his life."

"You mean all he did all day was work in a garden?"

"Yes. Leastways that was his profession. He also liked to play a fluty instrument called a jop in the evenings and take me and my sister fishing on rest days."

"Hmm." Miri tried to imagine the kind of life where fishing was a holiday game instead of a way to get food. "Not many gardens here."

Knut rubbed the gray in his beard. "Not many? I'd say not a one."

Miri felt her face go hot, and she was trying to think of something to say in defense of her mountain when Knut turned his smile to the window and said, "Not that you need them for scenery with these mountaintops taking your breath away."

And immediately Miri decided that Knut was the best sort of person. She asked him about gardens and the lowlands, heard about farms that stretched so far you had to ride a fast pony to get from one end to the other before noon, and the fancy gardens the rich had, full of plants just to look at instead of to eat. He taught her the names of several flowers and trees in the painting.

"My name is Miri, like the pink flower that grows around linder beds. Do you have miri flowers in the lowlands?"

"No, I think miri must be a mountain flower."

He startled at a sound from outside. "I should go." He looked out the door and around, as if checking to see if Olana were nearby, then leaned toward Miri and whispered, "I don't like the way she treats you. It should change." He gestured to the book in her hands. "Keep reading that one, Miri, and you won't be sorry."

So Miri sighed, sat down, and reopened *Danlander Commerce*. Even Olana's obscure lecture had been easier to understand. Olana had said that Commerce was the trading of one thing of value for another thing of value. The only thing of value on the mountain was linder, so Miri thumbed through the book, scanning for any mention of it. She found a passage in a chapter titled "Danlander Commodities."

> Of all the building stones, linder is most favored. It is hard enough to hold up great palaces and never crack, yet light enough to haul long distances. It is highly polishable, and linder one thousand years laid still gleams like new silver. Chapels must be made of wood, but a palace requires linder. In Danland, the only known beds of linder are found on Mount Eskel.

Miri brushed her fingertips over the passage. She had not known that linder was so rare. "That makes Mount Eskel important, even to lowlanders." She had always wished it so, and here was proof.

Olana had talked of supply and demand—if there was not much of a product available and demand was high, then that product would increase in value. It seemed to Miri that if linder was found only on Mount Eskel and yet prized enough to be used for palaces, then its value must be quite high. But how high? Near the back of the book she found a list.

Market Prices, Set by King's Treasurer
Bushel of wheat—one silver coin
Full-grown pig—three silver coins
Carriage horse—five silver coins or one gold coin

The list went on, giving the number of silver or gold coins for a cow, a load of timber, a plow horse, a good wagon. The last item on the list made Miri's heart pound. "Squared block of linder," it read. "One gold coin."

Just then the other girls entered the classroom.

"Look at Miri, still reading," said Katar.

"Huh? Oh, yes," Miri mumbled.

In the lowlands, one block of linder was worth five bushels of wheat. Five!

"Reading every book ten times won't be enough to make the prince choose you," said Katar.

"Maybe," said Miri, sliding the book onto the shelf.

One block of linder would be worth a fine horse,

finer than anything the traders hooked to their wagons.

"You don't need to act as if you've already won, Miri," said Bena.

"Indoor behavior," said Olana, entering, "or you'll take turns in the closet all night."

Miri took her seat, dizzy with her discovery. She stared at her feet, resting so casually on a floorstone of linder. She tried to estimate how many blocks of linder had been used to build the foundation of that building, how many bushels of grain it would buy, how much wood to build a chapel big enough to hold the whole village, enough food so no one's belly felt pinched on a winter's night, a library of books, spun cloth like the lowlanders wore, new shoes, musical instruments, sweets for the little ones, a comfortable chair for every grandparent, and a hundred other necessities and fancy things. If the traders dealt fairly, her village could benefit from the heaps of wonders the rest of the kingdom seemed to enjoy.

She could not wait to tell her pa and the other villagers. Soon now. Spring holiday was in two months, and by then the snow would break enough to make walking to the village possible. Surely Olana would allow them to return home for that celebration.

"Miri!"

Miri jumped at her name and realized belatedly

that Olana had spoken it several times.

"Yes, Tutor Olana?" she said, attempting to display meekness.

"It seems you haven't had time to contemplate the value of paying attention. You just lost your outdoor privileges for the rest of the week, and since that doesn't seem punishment enough, you are forbidden to touch the books for that period."

"Yes, Tutor Olana." In truth, Miri did not mind. Between quarry-speech and Commerce, she had plenty to think about.

Chapter Nine

Breathe, buzz, hint, spell
Sigh, speak, say, tell

Each day, each snowfall, each lesson until spring holiday felt endless, and Miri was sore and restless with waiting. Each night as she lay on her pallet, she held on to the thought that she was one night closer to telling her pa and the villagers about Commerce. All seemed to feel the anticipation of spring. Even Katar stared out the window as though measuring the snow depth with her eyes and counting the days until they could go home.

When Miri's punishment lapsed, she walked outdoors with Britta, explaining what they had to look forward to.

"Food," she said. "The best. Doter shares her honeyed nuts, and Frid's pa makes salted rabbit so thin it melts on your tongue. And hot tea with honey, the last of the apples salted and roasted, bread on a stick baked over a fire and seasoned with rabbit fat. Games and contests, and when the night comes we build bonfires from wood gathered all year and hold story shouts."

"Sounds lovely." Britta's faraway look said she was already imagining it.

"And it will be even better this year," said Miri. "I have some secrets."

Just by admitting she had them, the secrets pushed inside her, a snowmelt stream against a fallen branch, and the desire to share swept over her. She hesitated. Would Britta believe her? Or would she laugh? Miri thought of Doter's saying, *Never hesitate if you know it's right.* After months of ignoring Britta just for being a lowlander, at least she deserved Miri's trust.

So Miri took Britta on a frantic stroll around the academy, telling her with huffs of frosty breath about Commerce and gold coins and quarry-speech outside the quarry. Telling someone felt good, like drinking warmed goat's milk, and she rushed out every detail before Olana could call them back.

"That's the most amazing story I ever heard." Britta smiled, looking where the sun picked out stars on the icy husk of the snow. "What the traders are doing, that sounds dirty to me. We have to change that."

"So, you really never heard anyone using quarry-speech? Not even when you were working in the quarry?"

Britta shook her head. "Before coming up here, I never imagined such things could exist. It makes sense to me that mountain folk have that talent. I remember, the noise in the quarry was deafening, even with clay plugs in my ears."

"Up here, quarry-speech is as normal as bug bites. I don't suppose anyone's thought much about it."

Britta scratched her nose. "Maybe that was why I had a hard time at first, that and everyone is singing all the time. I could never join in because I don't know the words."

"You don't have to know the words, you just make up your own."

"But I don't know the tunes."

"You don't need to know the tunes, just find the rhythm and the song comes."

"I can't do that. I never learned how."

Miri had never realized that singing was something that needed to be learned. "Is it true what they say about lowlanders, that they have a way with growing things?"

"I've never heard that, but it is a lot greener down there." Britta looked west. "Less snow, more rain, green all along the seashore, and forests and farmlands for miles. Every house has its own garden."

"I'd like to see it sometime." It was awkward for

Miri to admit, but she did want to see the lowlands, the places she had imagined since she was a child and the things she had read about at the academy. The ocean, cities, palaces built of linder, musicians and artists, people from countries across the ocean, sailing ships full of wonders to sell and trade, a king and a queen. And a prince. Perhaps he would not be so horrible; perhaps he would be Britta's kind of lowlander.

"I'd like to see it with you," said Britta. "Someday. When you're the princess."

Miri laughed and pushed Britta's shoulder. "Maybe he'll choose you, Lady Britta. I mean, Princess Britta."

"No, not me. In a room full of girls, you and Liana and everybody, he won't even look at me."

"He will so—"

"It's all right, Miri," said Britta. "I don't care. It should be you or someone else really from Mount Eskel. I'm glad I got to attend the academy and meet you. That's the good part. Who cares about a prince, anyway?"

"I'd wager the prince himself cares a great deal," said Miri as they rushed back to the academy at Olana's call. "And he might have a puppy who is quite fond of him."

"The only thing I wish is that whoever does become the princess is happy, I mean really, really happy. Otherwise, what would it matter, right?"

Back in the classroom as Olana spouted the principles of Conversation Miri had already memorized, she let her mind wander, imagined marrying a prince who looked like Peder and lived in a palace of linder, and wondered if she would be, as Britta had said, really, really happy. Miri shook her head at the thought. Such a thing felt impossible, like her outlandish miri flower wishes, like trying to envision the ocean.

On the other hand, academy princess, with its immediate promise and silver gown, felt real, something she could daydream about.

In order to beat Katar as first in the academy, Miri knew she would have to be an expert on everything Olana taught. The lesson on Diplomacy had been vague and rushed, so the next rest day during personal study, Miri read a chapter on Diplomacy in *Danlander Commerce*, puzzling over the rules and how one might actually use them.

Esa sat in front of her, twirling a lock of hair the same shade as Peder's. Miri remembered the day Esa had gestured to her to come outside with the others. She had never explained about Olana and the closet and why she had not followed.

"Esa, what do you think this means?" Miri whispered, pointing to one of the general rules of Diplomacy—*Build on common ground*.

"I'm not sure." Esa took the book and read for a few minutes, flipping through several pages. "The book gives an example here, talking about a time when Danlanders first started to trade with eastern tribes who didn't speak our language. Before they could begin trading, they had to create relationships of trust, so they looked for things both peoples had in common." She paused to keep reading. "Listen to this—apparently a friendship between a Danlander and a chief of a tribe began when they discovered that both enjoyed eating roasted fish eyeballs. Ick. Funny way to start a friendship."

Miri smiled. "Didn't ours start when we were two years old and ate half of your ma's pot of butter under the table?"

Esa laughed and Katar shushed them. Miri frowned at Katar for spoiling the moment. She had always longed to be good friends with Esa, but Peder had never wanted his baby sister to tag along with them, and then as they grew up . . . Miri looked at the nineteen girls around her, bent over books and tablets, moving their lips as they read. It had been difficult to keep childhood friends while the others worked in the quarry and she was alone with the goats. But they were all together at the academy. If she wanted it, now was her chance.

"Thank you, Esa," Miri whispered.

Build on common ground. The question of quarry-speech was constantly murmuring in the back of Miri's mind, and the truth in this idea held her and pushed her thoughts deeper. Her questions had to wait until she could relax into her thinking time, in the bed-chamber after the hushed whispers and giggles of nighttime were replaced by snores and she felt safe, awake, and alone.

They didn't speak the same language, she thought, pondering the story Esa had read, *so they found other ways to communicate by sharing what they had in common.*

When Gerti had heard Miri's quarry-speech, she had remembered her own time in the closet. The thing they had in common—they had both experienced the closet and the scuttling noises of the rat.

Miri's thoughts began to buzz like flies over a meal. That last day before coming to the academy, Miri had heard Doter tell another quarry worker to lighten the blow. How had she known what Doter said? Thinking back to that moment, she realized she had imagined the time Marda had taught her how to pound a wheel of cheese and corrected her when she hit it too hard. The quarry-speech had prompted a real memory in her own mind, and she had interpreted the memory into what it might mean in that moment—*Lighten the blow.*

Quarry-speech used memories to carry messages.

Peder and her pa talked about quarry-speech as though it were second nature, and Miri guessed they did not realize how it worked and did not really care. But Miri did. The doings of the quarry had always seemed some bright, forbidden secret. Now it was her secret, and holding it to herself felt warm and delicious, like drinking the last cup of honeyed tea. She wanted to keep that feeling.

Chapter Ten

No wolf falters before the bite
So strike
No hawk wavers before the dive
Just strike

One more snowfall, then the clouds retreated higher than any mountain. Winter's grip eased, and the sun seemed to lean in closer to Mount Eskel. It was painfully bright, the sky a hot blue. The hard crust of snow softened and patches of earth emerged, showing green things rising out of the mud and pushing up onto the hills. The smell of the wind changed—it felt thicker, richer, like the air around a cook pot. Spring was stretching on the mountain.

More and more often, the girls looked up from their books and toward the heartening sight of Mount Eskel's peak, shedding white for brown and green. Miri could not think of returning home without a plummeting sensation in her belly. She hoped so powerfully to be able to share the secrets of Commerce and change trading for her village that she nearly trembled with it. Then, the day before they planned on making the trek for spring holiday, Olana announced a test.

"I know you think to return tomorrow," said Olana. "Your spring holiday is not a Danlander tradition, and this academy is under no obligation to honor it. Let the exam determine if you've earned the right to return home. Those who don't pass will remain at the academy, engaged in personal study."

The testing began with reading aloud, and Miri winced when Frid struggled with the big words and Gerti had no comprehension of the text on the page. Olana asked questions on History, Geography, and Kings and Queens, and the girls wrote out their answers on clay tablets. They walked across the room to exhibit Poise and conversed in pairs. Olana kept track of each girl's progress on a piece of parchment.

As painful as the testing was, Olana made it worse by declaring she would not give the scores until the next day.

"It will be good for you to ponder your performance until morning," said Olana.

In their bedchamber, Miri heard panicked whispering late into the night.

"I have to go home."

"Me too. No matter what."

"I know I failed. I'm sure I did. All the questions were so hard."

"She hates us. She'll fail us all just to be mean."

"Shush, or she'll fail us for talking."

The next morning, the girls sat so straight that they did not touch the backs of their chairs. The weight of Miri's desire to return home made her feel lopsided and giddy. *If Olana won't let me go*, she thought, *I may have to run.* But she was not ready to give up on the academy either, on all she was learning, on the hopes of becoming academy princess and being that special one, even on the rough and furtive yearning that she would not let herself think on too long—leaving the mountain, giving her pa the house in the painting, becoming a princess.

"Well," said Olana, facing the class with hands clasped behind her back. "Any guesses?"

No one answered.

"No need to drag it out," said Olana, and someone snorted at the comment. "You all failed."

A collective gasp went up.

"Except Miri and Katar."

Miri exchanged looks with Katar and saw that the other girl was pleased.

"You both may go." Olana waved them off.

Katar walked to the door and turned, waiting. Miri had not moved.

"Tutor Olana." Miri swallowed and spoke a little louder. "Tutor Olana, that doesn't seem fair."

"Passing the test doesn't give you freedom to speak out, Miri," said Olana. "Go this moment or forfeit your right to go at all. Now, the rest of you are miles behind where you should be, and I will not have you mortify me in front of the chief delegate and the prince. I will busy myself elsewhere in the building for the next couple of days. I'd rather not see much of you, which means I had better not *hear* much from you."

Miri had not left her seat. If she went with Katar, the others girls might never forgive her, but if she stayed, she could not deliver her news before the first trading of the season. She pressed her hands on her chair, wanting to stand, afraid to do so. Katar made exaggerated expressions of impatience by widening her eyes and tapping her foot.

Before Miri could make up her mind, Esa stood, her face a burning red. She clenched her left arm with her right hand.

"No," said Esa.

Olana turned her icy glare to Esa. "What was that?"

"I said . . . I said," Esa stuttered. She blinked many times, and tears began to leak from her eyes. "I said, no. I said, I'm going to spring holiday, and I don't care what happens."

Miri stared at Esa and felt as breathless as if she had fallen on her back. Esa was the one girl who had never missed a meal or received a palm lashing, always holding her tongue, always obedient.

Miri could see no hope in Esa's face. She seemed to cringe, waiting for the inevitable punishment, knowing she would never be allowed to leave but unable to stop her protest.

Never hesitate if you know it's right. Miri was going to spring holiday, and she wanted everyone to go with her. If they ran all at once, she believed Olana and the soldiers could not stop them.

"A few hours in the closet might chill the impudence out of you," Olana was saying.

Miri knew she had to act before Olana called the soldiers or locked Esa up. After months of cold tension, she was afraid she could not convince the girls to run home. Besides, she would not be able to talk for long before Olana would have the soldiers haul her away. No, her gut told her that the only way to communicate her plea to run was to use quarry-speech.

She did not know if it was possible to say something

so specific; she had never tried. But if quarry-speech used memories, could she convey more than just quarry warnings? Could she tell everyone to run?

Miri stomped her foot on the linder floorstones and sang out loud, hoping to distract Olana from taking Esa to the closet. "No wolf falters before the bite. So strike. No hawk wavers before the dive. Just strike." It was a song for wedge work, when every stroke was critical. If any quarrier in the line delayed a strike, the crack could split the wrong way and ruin the linder block. There could be no hesitation.

Olana gaped at Miri stomping and singing. That made Miri laugh.

"That's enough," said Olana.

"No sun pauses before the set, so swing," Miri sang on, while her thoughts dashed around, trying to find a common memory that would encourage all the girls to run at once. "No rain delays before the fall. Just swing." Then she had it—Rabbit and Wolf, a game all villagers knew. The children would sit in a circle and the child who was the "wolf" chased the "rabbit" around the outside of the circle, trying to touch her hair. If the wolf touched the rabbit anywhere else, it was an unfair touch. The rabbit yelled, "Rabbits, run!" and all the children stood and ran.

Miri seized this memory and sang it with her

thoughts, down into the beating of her boot, down into the linder.

The sight of Olana shivered, and her memory of the game expanded, seeming immediate and clear. Half the girls stood right up, and the rest flinched or jumped or shook their heads as if trying to jiggle water out of their ears. Only Britta and Olana did not react.

"What is going on?" Olana looked around. She seemed too bewildered by the odd behavior to know what to do. "Why are you standing?"

Again Miri sang the memory in quarry-speech, and the rest of the girls stood. Even Bena and Katar had knowing smiles on their faces. Miri took Britta's arm and whispered, "We're going home now."

Despite her tears, Esa grinned. "Rabbits, run."

Some of the girls squealed with delight and fear as they darted out of the classroom and dashed down the steps.

Behind them, Olana bellowed, "If you leave now, don't think about coming back! Do you hear me?"

They laughed as they ran. It was still morning, and the chilly air of early spring nipped and butted Miri's skin. She would make it home. She would have a chance to tell her pa about Commerce. She wanted to hug the whole world.

"Shouldn't we hurry?" asked Gerti, looking over her shoulder. "What if the soldiers catch us?"

"One of us is going to be the princess one day," said Miri. "What can they do, run us all through with their swords?"

Thirteen-year-old Jetta shrieked, and the others laughed at her fright. The soldiers did not follow, and the girls slowed to a walk, talking over everything they must have missed at home these last months and all that they would do for spring holiday. Miri took Britta's hand, and Esa and Frid walked with them.

"I guess we've being playing Wolf and Rabbit with Olana all along," said Miri, "but when she picks on Esa, that's an unfair touch. I'm glad we ran."

"So am I," said Esa. "I was in the closet for sure."

"And it's time that rat's reign of terror ended." Miri stole a sideways glance at Esa, then looked back at the road. "I never apologized for getting everyone in trouble, and then I was too embarrassed to speak up. I thought you wouldn't forgive me, but I am sorry."

Frid's eyes widened. "Oh. I thought all along you were mad at us."

"You did?"

"You always stayed inside reading and didn't talk to us. I guessed you were angry that we didn't take your side against Katar."

Miri laughed, pleased. "And I thought you were too angry to talk to me."

"Miri, I'm dying to know," said Esa. "That was you who quarry-spoke back there, wasn't it? It felt like you. But how did you do it? I've never heard anyone say, 'Rabbits, run!' before, and outside the quarry!"

They were walking through a quarry some hundred years deserted, but patches of linder too thin to mine still gleamed through the mud and rock shards. Miri crouched on a lean slab, tapped the rhythm with her fist, and chose a memory. At age three, she and Esa had wriggled out of Doter's notice and scampered dangerously close to the cliff's edge. "Take care!" Doter had shouted before pulling them to safety. *Take care*, Miri now quarry-spoke.

Frid's mouth hung open, and Esa nodded and smiled.

"I didn't think it was possible outside our quarry," said Frid.

"What did you just see?" asked Miri.

"See?" asked Esa. "What do you mean? I heard a warning about being careful and coming away from an edge."

"But does anything else occur to you? A memory of anything?" Miri rapped again, sang aloud, and sang inside.

"I guess one time when you and I almost fell off the cliff and my ma pulled us back."

"Me too!" said Miri. "But what does it remind you of, Frid?"

"When Os was on a block high in the quarry, and I saw him lose his balance and fall."

Miri clapped her hands together. "It must be true. I've been thinking that quarry-speech works in memories. If two people have the same memory, like Esa and me, then we might imagine the same scene. But if not, then the quarry-speech nudges the nearest memory."

"Maybe that's why lowlanders can't hear it," said Britta. "We don't have enough shared memories."

"I've been trying to figure out quarry-speech for months," said Miri, "but I still don't know why it sometimes works outside the quarry and sometimes not."

Esa shielded her eyes to spot the rest of the girls walking on the road ahead. "Let's think about it later. I'm dying for some honeyed nuts."

The four girls skipped to catch up with the others and hollered spring songs all the way home.

Chapter Eleven

I'll raise the ladle to your lips,
Drip water on your fingertips,
And stay although my heart says flee.
Will you look up and smile at me?

That afternoon, the sounds of song greeted them at the outskirts of the village. Dozens of voices carried the melody, and slapping drums and clapping hands thrummed the beat. The girls recognized the tune and rhythm of the empty barrel dance, the first dance of spring holiday.

"Hurry up," said Esa. "They'll need us, or most of the boys will be dancing alone."

The girls broke into a run, and the noise of their boots on the roadway sounded like a night rockfall.

"We're here, we're back!" some shouted, and when they came into view of the village center, a cheer went up. The clapping broke from its dance rhythm into applause for their entrance, and parents and siblings shouted and leaped forward to embrace them. Miri looked for Marda and her father and was about to despair when they rushed her from behind.

Her pa lifted her in the air and spun her around as if she were still a little girl. Marda was there as well, kissing her cheeks and warming her cold hands. Miri's eyes felt watery, and she put her face against her pa's chest.

"Are you all right?" asked Marda.

She nodded, still hiding her face. "I just missed you all. I guess I missed you a lot."

The holiday was the best in Miri's memory. Frid beamed so proudly when she took first place the stone-hurling contest, she seemed to forget that she had won every year since she was twelve. The food was better than Miri could ever have described to Britta, and the cheering never really died out. Everything seemed worthy of applause.

Frid's pa announced the ribbon dances with a strum of his three-stringed yipper, and Doter handed out the tattered red strips of cloth that were older than any grandparent. Jans, a pale, serious boy, trailed Britta around like a thistleweed stuck to her bootlace. He begged her for one more dance, and then one more, so for an hour she shared her ribbon with Jans, high stepping and twisting and smiling wider than Miri had ever seen.

Miri herself danced so hard that she could scarcely breathe. She saw Peder dancing with Bena and then Liana and had given up hoping when a new song began and she found him on the other end of her ribbon. She would have talked and teased and laughed with him, but his sudden appearance had startled her, and she did not know if she could keep up her carefree façade. Her gaze fell on the ground, her heart beating faster than the drums.

After a time, she did not see Peder anymore among the dancers, and she nestled close to her father and watched the toddlers twirl and hop. When night fell the story shouts began. The grandfathers told the somber story of the creator god first speaking to people; then the mothers recited the one that began, "One lifetime ago bandits came to Mount Eskel."

After the bandit story, Os said, "Let's hear a tale from our girls come home."

Bena, as the oldest, stood and chose her story, a silly romp of a tale where each line was invented as it was told. "The girl with no hair left home to wander hills where she was not known," she shouted, then pointed to Liana, who sat at another fire.

"An eagle mistook her for her fallen egg and carried her up to its nest," shouted Liana, pointing to Frid.

"A quarrier plucked her from the eagle's nest, thinking her a good stone to break." Frid pointed to Gerti.

The story continued, each academy girl selecting another to continue the tale. Miri inched up to sit on her heels, hoping to be seen. No one looked her way. Bena had three turns, and even Britta was chosen once, inventing a clever line about a bear mistaking her for a mushroom cap. Then Esa shouted, "Last line!" and pointed to Miri.

Miri stood, her smile impossible to hide. "With her bald head shining like a gold crown, a wandering prince mistook her for an academy princess and carried her away to his palace."

The crowd burst into cheers and laughter.

The festivities slowed and families clustered around fires, drinking tea, with honey if they were lucky, and singing sleepy tunes. Miri's gaze wandered over the faces lit by the bonfires until she discovered Peder just beyond the ring of orange light.

Miri had not spoken a word to him since returning, and she realized now that she might have seemed unfriendly while they danced. She should have run to him at once and told him all her news. Instead she had held back, embarrassed. She stood to go to him, then hesitated.

Don't hesitate if you know it's right, Miri reminded herself. *Just swing.*

Her palms were hot, and she clenched her fists and tried to think of what she would say. In her distress, her mind clung to the Conversation lessons. *Repeat his name. Ask questions. Make observations, not judgments. Return the conversation to him.* And something Britta had added: *If you want to impress someone, act as though they are your better.*

"Hi, Peder," said Miri, approaching where he sat alone. "How have you been?"

"All right, thanks." His voice was short, as if he did not want to speak with her. She almost ran away then. Being near him made her insides feel like twisted vines, choking and blooming at the same time, and her only clear thought was that his smile was worth trudging for.

"May I sit with you?"

"Sure."

She sat beside him on a cut linder block, careful not to let her leg touch his. "I'd like to hear about . . . how things have been . . . lately."

"Fine enough. A little quieter than usual without Esa in the house."

She continued to pose questions, using his name, making eye contact, making sure her mannerisms showed she was wholly focused on him. After a time, his responses got longer. Soon she had him talking freely about how that winter had been the bleakest he had known.

"Never thought I'd miss my little sister," he said playfully. "Esa . . . and all the girls."

Miri wondered, *Is he thinking of Bena or Liana?*

He glanced at Miri, then back at his hands. "I never thought that every day of working the quarry could get any worse."

"What do you mean, worse? Don't you like the mountain? You wouldn't rather be a lowlander."

"No, of course not." He picked up a linder shard from beside her boot. "I don't mind quarry work, really, but sometimes my head gets tired of it, and I want to . . . I'd like to make things, not just cut stone. I want to do work that I'm really good at, that feels just right."

It chilled Miri to hear him speak so openly, and thoughts so like her own. Instead of shouting, "*Me too! That's how I feel!*" she remembered the rules of Conversation and stayed focused on him. "If you could do anything in the world, what would it be?"

He thought a moment, opened his mouth, then shrugged and tossed the shard away. "Never mind, it's nothing."

"Peder Doterson, you had best tell me now. I'll hold my breath until I know."

He picked up a new linder shard and examined its color. Miri waited for him to speak.

"It doesn't really matter, but I've always . . . You know the carvings on the chapel doors? I've stared and stared at them the way I see you sometimes watch the sky." He looked over her face as if he were studying the carvings. His look stilled her. "As long as I can remember, I've wanted to make things like that, something more than blocks of stone. I sometimes . . . You promise not to laugh at me?"

Miri nodded earnestly.

"You know how I carve little things from thrown-off linder?"

"Yes," she said, "you made me a goat once. I still have it."

He smiled. "You do? I remember that goat. He had a crooked smile."

"A perfect smile," said Miri. It had always reminded her of Peder's.

"It's probably childish, but I like making things like that. Linder shapes really well, better than rubble rock. I'd like to make designs in the blocks, things rich lowlanders might buy to have over doorways or above their hearth."

The idea caught Miri's breath, it was so perfect. "Why don't you?"

"If Pa ever found me making stone pictures, he'd whip me for wasting time. We barely cut enough linder each year to trade for food, and it doesn't seem likely that anything will ever change."

"It might." She meant for the comment to slip unnoticed, but something in her tone must have intrigued him.

"How?" he asked.

Miri shrugged off the question. It was going too well to give up on the rules of Conversation now. He pressed again, wanting to hear about what she had been doing at the academy all winter, and again she tried to keep talking about him.

Peder sighed in frustration. "Why are you being so evasive? Tell me, I really want to know."

Miri hesitated, but his attention was irresistible, and she had a thousand stories trembling on her tongue. Then he smiled in his way, the right side of his mouth curving higher. She rubbed his tawny curls as she might her favorite nanny goat after a milking.

"You may be sorry you asked," she said, and drowned him with the account of the last few months, telling all from getting her palms lashed and the first snowfall to their escape from the school earlier that day. She spoke quickly, her tongue feeling like a hummingbird's wing; she was so afraid of boring him if she took too long. Then she described how she had been experimenting with quarry-speech, how she could share a memory, not just deliver a warning, and how it sometimes worked outside the quarry.

"Though it sometimes doesn't." She lifted her hand to say she did not know why.

"Try it right now."

Miri swallowed. Quarry-speaking with Esa and Frid had felt like a game, but with Peder it became something intimate, like reaching for his hand, like looking into his eyes even when she had nothing to say. Hoping she was not blushing, she rapped her knuckles on the linder block and sang about a girl who carried drinking water in the quarry. She let the song guide her and began to match her thoughts to its rhythm, searching for a good memory to use, when Peder stopped her with a smile.

"What are you doing?"

Now she did blush, cursing herself for choosing a song about a love-struck girl. "I'm . . . I thought you said to try to quarry-speak."

"Yes, but you know you don't have to pound and sing, right?" Peder waited for her to agree, but she just stared. "You know that in the quarry we happen to be pounding and singing while we work, but that we can use quarry-speech without doing all that."

"Yes, of course," she said, smiling. "Of course I knew that. Only an idiot would think you have to pound the stone to make quarry-speech after all."

"Yes, of course." He laughed, and she laughed back, bumping him with her shoulder. Peder had always been good about letting her mistakes slide.

"So you don't have to pound, and the only singing happens inside." She splayed her hand on the stone and without a song quarry-spoke to Peder. It felt like whispering something right to his heart. When her vision shuddered, she shivered as well.

"That was strange." Peder looked at her. "Is that what you mean by memories? It felt like quarry-speech, but I'm used to hearing the warnings we use as we work. This time, I was just thinking about the afternoon when I made that linder goat." His eyes widened as his thoughts seemed to race forward. "Is it because you spoke a memory? One that I knew, one that I lived, so it was so clear to me . . . Miri, that's amazing."

"I wonder why it worked now. . . ." Miri smoothed her hand over the stone. The linder was chipped and irregular and pocked with chisel marks, not smooth like the polished floorstones of the academy. She lifted her fingers to her mouth and pressed them against her growing smile. A new idea sent her spinning. "Peder, I think I understand. I think it's the linder."

"What's the linder? What do you mean?"

She stood up, feeling as though the idea were too big to crouch inside her and needed room to stretch. "The academy floor is made of linder, so is this stone, and the whole quarry . . . you see? Those other times when it didn't work, I must have been outside or on rubble rock. Maybe quarry-speech works best around linder."

"Sit back down and let me try." He yanked her arm and she sat beside him. This time she was a little closer, the sides of their legs touching.

He closed his eyes, the muscles of his forehead tense. Miri held her breath. For a time nothing happened. Then she found her thoughts flash to that afternoon on the grazing hill, the scrape of Peder's knife on a shard of linder, a plaited miri chain dangling from her fingers. It was her own memory, but stronger, vivid, pulled forward to the front of her thoughts, and full of color. And she knew it was Peder speaking that memory, the way she knew the smell of baking bread—it had the sense of him.

"I couldn't figure it out at first," he said. "I'm so used to repeating the quarry warnings we always use."

"You told me once that quarry-speech was like

singing inside, and that's how I knew what to do."

"Huh," he said, shaking his head. "A lot has happened while you were away."

"I'd tell you more if I thought I could do it before sunup."

"I'm sure you would. It must have been very hard to keep quiet all those weeks."

Miri punched his shoulder.

"I can imagine you at the academy window, looking off toward the village," he said, "believing you could see it if you just looked hard enough. You always were a hawk, gazing at the mountains as if you could see a mouse running on a far hill, or at the sky as if you could count every feather on a sparrow's wing."

Miri did not respond. She felt as though she were floating underwater, tipping and sinking. Did he watch her just as she watched him?

"I've never told anyone about carving stone," he said. "I don't know how you got it out of me."

Miri laughed. "Because I'm pushier than a billy goat mad. I won't tell anyone else."

"I know you won't. I know that about you." He held the end of her braid and brushed it across his palm. He frowned as if a new thought occurred to him. "Do you ever wear your hair loose?"

"Sometimes." Her voice creaked, but her mouth was too dry to swallow. "I did last year at autumn holiday."

"That's right." His expression was distant, as if he were remembering. "I miss all the time we had when we were younger, don't you? It'd be nice to go exploring the peak again, maybe on rest days."

"It would." Miri held very still, afraid that if she moved she might spook Peder and like a lone wolf he would suddenly run off. "When I'm not at the academy anymore."

Peder let go of her braid, but Miri still could not quite catch her breath. He turned his hands over, as if looking for something he lost.

"The academy. So, you might marry the prince?"

"Oh, I don't know," said Miri, just then discovering that she was sore from sitting so long. "I'm trying to do my best in the class so maybe he'd notice me. I mean, he'd have to choose me from all the other girls . . . and I'm not trying *not* to be the princess or anything. It's just . . . he won't pick me."

"Why not?" said Peder. "I mean, why wouldn't he? You're the smartest one in the class."

"I didn't mean to make it sound like that—"

"Well, I bet you are," interrupted Peder, his voice rising. "And if he's half a prince he'll see that and then want to carry you off to the lowlands to put you in fancy dresses. But I don't think you need to wear lowlander dresses. You're just fine." He stood. "Never mind. I should get back to my family."

Miri wanted to say something that mattered before he walked away. She blurted, "I won't tell anyone about your stone carving. But I think it's wonderful, and I think you're wonderful."

He stood there, letting the silence stretch thinner and thinner until Miri's panicked heart left her with nothing more than burning cheeks.

"You're my best friend, you know," he said.

Miri nodded.

"I wish I had something to give you, some welcome home." He patted the pocket of his shirt, as if looking for anything at all.

"It's all right, Peder, you don't have to—"

Swiftly he stooped, kissed her cheek, and disappeared.

Miri did not move for three verses of the next bonfire song. A smile tugged at one corner of her mouth like a brook trout on a fishing line, but she was too staggered to give in to it.

"That went well," she whispered to herself, and then did smile.

"What are you grinning about?" Britta sat beside her, mirroring Miri's happy expression.

"Nothing," said Miri, but she could not help looking where Peder had gone, and Britta followed her glance.

"Oh." Britta laughed. *"Nothing."*

Miri laughed in return and felt her face go hot again, and it occurred to her that after so much burning her cheeks should be ashes by now. She quickly changed the subject. "What do you like best so far—the food, stories, dancing, or a certain smitten boy by the name of Jans?"

Britta shook her head, refusing to acknowledge Miri's pointed question. "It's all wonderful. I think this is better than any lowlander party."

Miri elbowed her. "Look at how you say 'lowlander' as if you were a mountain girl."

"I'd like to be," said Britta.

"Then you are," said Miri. "That's the only ceremony you need."

The drums and singing died out, and Gerti's father, Os, called for village council. The youth moved away from the bonfires to leave the business to the older folks. An excited rumble in her stomach reminded Miri that she had something to present.

"Come on, Britta, I may need your help."

Miri had never attended council before. She sat beside her pa, her head on his shoulder, Britta by her side. The talk concerned recent linder blocks cut, an injury of a stone braker due to carelessness, the most promising parts of the quarry to undertake next, and the use of supplies over the winter.

"But no matter how much linder we cut, Os, it won't be enough," said Peder's father. "The absence of the girls meant fewer hands to help. My own boy has had to care more for the goats and the home, and that's one less stone this season. Isn't that right, Laren?"

Miri's father nodded. "I feel the pinch this year."

Miri rose. "I have something to say."

Her father raised his brows but did not speak, and Os indicated that she go ahead. Miri hummed her throat clear.

"At the academy, I found a book that explains how linder is sold in the lowlands. Apparently, our stone is so prized that the king himself will only use linder for his palaces, and the only place in all of Danland that produces linder is right here. So because demand for linder is high and supply is limited, it's worth a great deal."

She glanced at her pa to see if he approved. He was listening, but his expression betrayed no opinion. Miri cleared her throat again.

"In the rest of the kingdom, they trade for gold or silver coins instead of just food and supplies. In the capital, a block of linder is worth one gold coin, and in turn a gold coin can buy five bushels of wheat."

She paused, waiting for exclamations, but no one spoke. Then her pa touched her arm.

"Miri," he said softly.

"I know I'm asking you to believe a lowlander book, but I believe it, Pa. Why would a lowlander write anything good about Mount Eskel unless it was true?"

Britta spoke up. "Miri showed me the book, and I think it's true as well."

Os shook his head. "It's easy to believe the traders will cheat us as much as they can, but what can we do about it?"

"Refuse to trade for anything but gold or silver, and at decent prices," said Miri. "Then if they don't haul enough goods to trade for our cut linder, we can take their money down the mountain to buy even more."

"There's a large market in a town three days from here," said Britta. "We stayed at an inn on my journey last summer. Gold and silver there would buy you much more than what the traders bring to your village."

Os rubbed his beard. "I can see the value in trading elsewhere, but if the traders won't take our linder for gold . . ."

"If they won't," said Doter, her eyes brightening,

"we threaten to take the linder down the mountain. If we trade linder in that market ourselves, we'll earn even more."

"No, no," said Katar's father. "We don't have the wagons or mules, and we don't know the first thing about a town marketplace. What if we drag all our blocks there and no one buys? What if in the process we offend the traders and they never return?"

The fear in that argument hushed all the talk. Miri curled her toes in her boots and made herself speak up again.

"I don't think the likes of Enrik would let it go that far. I really believe the traders are making heaps of money from our stone. They'll know we could sell the linder for more in the lowlands, and then they would be cut out of any profit." Miri looked again at her father and tried to stamp down the trembling hope in her voice. "What do you think, Pa?"

He nodded slowly. "I think it's worth the risk."

A sigh of relief dragged out of Miri's chest.

The idea sparked talk that did not die down until the flames dwindled into embers. The adults debated every angle, how to go about it, what risks they faced. They consulted Britta on anything she knew of trade. Some were concerned that the villagers could not tell true silver and gold from any cheap metal the traders might try to give them.

"My father was a merchant. I can make sure they don't cheat you," said Britta. "But what if the king gets impatient for the linder, and he sends men up here to quarry the stone themselves?"

Several chuckled at her question.

"If all lowlanders have arms as skinny as the traders do," said Frid's pa, "they'll have to rest between each mallet strike."

Miri folded her own skinny arms under her cloak.

"That's one thing we don't have to worry about, Britta," said Doter. "Let them come, and they'll give up after their first block cracks. We have linder in our bones."

The discussion continued, and Miri leaned into her pa, drowsy from watching the fire. He patted her hair. *We have linder in our bones*, Doter had said. *We*. Miri clung to the word, wanting to be a part of it but unsure if she was. If her idea for trading became a success, perhaps then she could be more certain.

Her gaze wandered from the gold flames to the darkness the firelight could not reach. Peder might be there, listening, hoping for a chance to carve stone.

Chapter Twelve

Mud in the stream
And earth in the air
Clay in my ears
And stone in my stare

It was not quite morning when Miri woke to the comforting sound of her pa's snore. She picked out the familiar shapes of the hearthstones, the door, the table, and breathed in the warm smell of home.

When dawn began to spark color into her dark house, Miri wrapped herself in her blanket and slipped outside to start breakfast. A dozen others were in the village center using the remains of last night's bonfires to heat that morning's meal. Miri settled her kettle of water into the coals and noticed some academy girls there as well. Their expressions were solemn in the gray morning.

"Are we going back?" asked Miri.

"That's what I've been wondering," said Esa.

Britta sat beside Miri. "Even if we want to, would Olana let us?"

"If she does," said Frid, "we might spend the summer taking turns in the closet."

"Olana said I could go to spring holiday, so I won't be punished," said Katar as she joined them. "I'm definitely going back."

Several other academy girls arrived, and they sat on stones in a crooked circle, watched the embers fizz and sputter against the dew, and talked of returning. Some were eager to go back, others too content the morning after a spring holiday to think of ever leaving. Katar and Bena were adamant.

"I won't have any of you risking my chances by breaking apart the academy," said Katar.

"The prince might choose someone else, Katar," said Bena. "I'd not thought much about him until last night I realized how dull all the village boys are. I'll bet a prince is interesting."

Liana nodded, ever echoing Bena's opinion. Miri wondered what Peder did last night to lose their interest so decisively. She imagined a spot on her cheek warmer than the rest.

"Miri fancies herself the one he'll choose," said Bena. "That's why she studies so hard, but she's too proud to admit it."

"How can you want to marry someone you've never met?" said Miri.

"What if you meet him and do like him, Miri?" Esa asked. "What if we all do?"

Frid frowned as though she thought that unlikely. Katar smirked, Bena stared at the morning stars, and three of the younger girls whispered to one another. Miri tried to keep her face unreadable. She had already fallen in love with the house in the painting, but after last night, the idea of Peder was too near and too full of hope to imagine marrying a prince.

"What's his name, anyway?" asked Gerti, settling her kettle in the coals.

"Steffan," said Britta.

"How did you know that?" asked Liana.

Britta shrugged. "Everyone knows down there."

"Everyone knows down there," said Katar in a high, mocking voice.

Britta blushed.

"Well done," said Miri, jumping in to save her friend. "So it's Steffan. Hm, sounds feeble to me. Bet he can't toss a pebble five paces."

Frid gasped, then roared with such laughter that it seemed nothing had struck her as so funny as the thought that someone would not be able to toss a pebble five paces. Miri half chuckled as well but felt uncomfortable laughing at her own joke, especially as no one else seemed to find it amusing at all.

"It doesn't matter if any of us fall in love with the prince," said Katar. "We should still return to the academy."

"I didn't realize how important the lowlanders considered the academy until we studied Danlander political structure," said Esa. "Before, I didn't know what a chief delegate was or why it was significant that he himself came to Mount Eskel with the news."

"What are you talking about?" asked Gerti's friend Jetar.

"Every province of Danland has a delegate," said Katar, yawning to show that she thought Jetar's ignorance very boring. "Every delegate represents them at court, and the chief delegate is head of them all. Second only to the king. He must've been pretty annoyed that we didn't realize how important he was."

Miri nodded with mock seriousness. "Ah yes, I remember well his marvelous feathered hat."

"No wonder lowlanders don't think of us as being true Danlanders," said Esa, "since Mount Eskel is just a territory."

"Maybe we shouldn't have run away," said Gerti.

"If the academy is that important, if we're that important . . ."

"And remember the lesson on Danlander Law?" said Katar. "And the punishments for disobeying the king?"

Frid folded her arms. "They might try to haul our fathers to Asland."

"We could get our parents to talk to Olana and explain . . . ," said Gerti.

"I think Olana might respect us more if we made things right on our own," said Esa. Her voice softened. "And I'd like to return. Even if I'll never be a princess, I'd like to learn more."

Miri rose to her feet with an idea. "If one of us really will be the princess, how can Olana push us around? She might be sticking her future queen in the closet to snuggle with a rat."

Katar scrunched her lips. "That is something to bargain with."

"Let's go back and show her we're smarter than she thinks." Miri paced with excitement. "Olana didn't spend much time on Diplomacy, but we learned enough to come up with a decent plan."

Bena rolled her eyes. "You think we can just hop into her lap, spout a bunch of Diplomacy rules, and that will make everything all better?"

"I wish I'd known the rules for Diplomacy that day Olana gave me a palm lashing," said Miri. "I think I could've argued my way out of it. It might be fun to try."

"Yes, and Miri should be the one to speak for us," said Gerti, patting her shoulder.

Katar, Bena, and Liana talked over one another, saying that one of the older girls should do it, that the matter was too delicate to leave to Miri.

"She's the one who got us in trouble before," said Bena.

Esa shrugged. "Olana said Miri scored best at the exam. And besides, using Diplomacy was her idea."

Britta and a few other girls voiced their support as well.

"It was Miri's idea," Frid said simply, and the disputing ceased. Frid's large, brawny family could eat a village's winter food supply and still feel hungry, yet they always donated some of their cut linder to smaller families, without fuss and without thanks. Even Bena would not argue with Frid.

Miri only nodded, but she felt like shouting. They trusted her. It gave her hope that at the academy, far from the quarry, she might have a chance to be as useful as everyone else.

By the time dawn put an orange haze around

Mount Eskel's crown, they had informed the other academy girls of their plan and returned home to spend the rest day with their families.

After their morning visit to the chapel, Miri's family stayed around the house doing idle chores. Marda and Pa wanted to know everything she had learned, and Miri did not need to wait for their questions to tell them.

Their house had a dirt floor, so she took them on a walk just beyond the village. They sat on a large linder block marred with a crack through its center, and Miri spoke to them in quarry-speech, at first just *Take care*, then a memory of the three of them roasting apples at the hearth while a winter storm thundered outside.

"Quarry-speech is just for the quarry," said Pa.

"I think it takes linder to work, not the quarry," said Miri.

Pa's cheeks wrinkled in a smile as though he thought she were making a joke. "Now what use would it be anywhere else?"

"Well, I think you can communicate more than just the quarry warnings. I guess you could say almost anything, as long as there's a memory that fits it."

Pa frowned, not understanding. Miri's heart sank. She had paced with impatience to come home and tell her father about Commerce and quarry-speaking. Now she asked herself what she had truly expected. That he would throw her in the air and declare she was smarter than he had thought and worthy to work by his side?

"I guess it wouldn't be interesting to a quarrier," said Miri. "I guess it's just interesting to me. Never mind."

"Can Britta hear it?" asked Marda.

"No," said Miri. "I don't think any lowlanders can."

Marda was staring off toward the quarry, and she began to sing a chiseling song. "'Mud in the stream, and earth in the air. Clay in my ears, and stone in my stare. Grit on my tongue, and dust in my hair. Inside and out, mountain everywhere.' I was just thinking, Pa, if lowlanders can't hear quarry-speech and it works with linder . . ."

Their father nodded. "Linder's in our blood and bones."

"You think it works for us because we live around linder?" asked Miri.

"And drink it and breathe it, all our lives." Marda ducked her head as if she wanted to be silent, but clearly the idea fascinated her, and she continued. "If it works around linder, and mountain folk have linder inside us . . . maybe linder shapes quarry-speech in the way that cupping your hands around your mouth makes your voice louder. Or maybe quarry-speech travels through linder like sound through air, and the more linder the louder it is. Our memories move through linder, whether in the mountain or in a person."

Miri stared at Marda. "You're smart," she said.

Marda shook her head and clamped her mouth shut.

Before the academy, Miri never had cause to wonder if a person was head smart or not. It seemed everyone was clever at something—there were those who were best at picking out the right fissure for prying a block of linder free and those who were best at making cheese or tanning hides, beating drums, or tossing stones. Now, smart meant to Miri the talent to think around a new problem and to learn new things.

And Marda was smart. It was injustice and not luck at all that made Marda three months too old to attend the academy. And not just Marda—what about the younger girls? And all the boys?

"I wish you could attend the academy," said Miri.

Marda shrugged, and the last hope in her expression hinted that she had daydreamed about the academy on many a winter night.

Pa seemed to sense that sadness had crept in, so he

ushered them back home to make oat biscuits for the last of the winter honey, saying, "A little honey can cheer the gloom out of bones and stones."

As they celebrated over biscuits, Miri joked and laughed despite her father's disappointing reaction, but her thoughts kept returning to Marda. She had never imagined that her sister yearned to be at the academy, perhaps as much as Miri longed to be welcome in the quarry. Miri snuck Marda an extra helping of honey when her back was turned and wished she could think of something that would make it right.

Chapter Thirteen

All I know are
Scraps, flakes, chips, rocks
All below are
Stones, shards, bits, dross

The next morning the girls walked back to the academy. This time no soldiers pressed them from behind, but Miri guessed she was not the only one feeling jittery. They talked over their Diplomacy strategy, and many of the girls offered ideas. Frid and other sixteen-year-olds were vocal and supportive, but Bena refused to speak again after she declared that Miri would fail, and Katar stayed in her usual spot alone at the head of the group.

When they arrived at the academy, the girls arranged themselves before the steps in a straight line. Miri could see Knut peering through a window.

In the silence of waiting, Miri became aware of the jagged rocks poking through her boot soles. They had already been thin when they had been Marda's, and now they were . . . Miri tried to think of a word that was thinner than "thin." She wanted to hop around or say something funny to relieve the nervous tension, but she was the diplomat and thought she had better appear respectable.

Finally Olana emerged, fists on her hips. The two soldiers stood behind her.

Miri brought to mind the first rule of diplomatic negotiations: *State the problem.* "We know we are not welcome inside," she said.

Olana blinked. That was not what she had been expecting to hear.

"We left without your permission and violated your authority," said Miri. The second rule: *Admit your own error.* "That was wrong."

Frid shuffled her feet nervously. Miri knew the girls had not been expecting to concede fault, but she was not confident she could be convincing without help from the rules of Diplomacy. Besides, she wanted Olana to see that they had listened and learned.

"You kept us from our families, punished us for unfair reasons, and treated us like criminals. That was also wrong. We're here now, willing to forget our mutual offenses and start over. Here are our terms."

Olana blinked rapidly, a sign that her composure had slipped. Miri felt encouraged. She reviewed the other rules: *State the error of the other party.* Done. *Propose specific compromises* and end with *Invite mutual acceptance.* She hoped she was not forgetting anything.

"For each rest day, we will be allowed to return home to our families and attend chapel, leaving in the late afternoon and then returning by rest day evening. When traders come, we will return home for one week to help barter, haul stone, and work in our homes. Rule breaking may be punished with a missed meal, but no one will be hit, locked in a closet, or grounded from a return home."

Olana clicked her tongue to show that she was not impressed. "I have a steep task to turn twenty mountain girls into presentable ladies. These measures are the only way I can keep you in line."

Miri nodded. "Perhaps they were, but no longer. As part of these new terms, we will vow to focus on our studies, respect your authority, and obey all reasonable rules." Just one more: *Illustrate the negative outcome of refusal and positive of acceptance.* "If you don't agree to this, whichever of us the prince chooses will report your bad behavior and demand of him that you serve the rest of your days in some outlying territory of Danland even more distasteful to you than Mount Eskel."

"A swamp," Britta whispered. Miri nodded. She had

read about a territory that was swampland—smelly, sticky with mud, and poorer than the mountains.

"Such as a swamp," said Miri.

Olana cringed visibly.

"And if you live by these terms and treat us as you would treat noblemen's daughters, whichever one of us chosen as the princess will commend your teaching and see you get comfortable work tutoring in Asland.

"As well, we request the dismissal of the soldiers. Their only purpose seems to be to intimidate us, so they should go home to Asland when the traders come again in a few weeks."

Olana arched one eyebrow. "In this very class we've read of bandits who rove the isolated territories of Danland. What will we do if they decide they like the look of Mount Eskel?"

Frid chuckled and the girls exchanged smiles. The tale of defeated bandits was a staple at spring holiday.

"Bandits did attack our village before I was born," said Katar, jumping in. "You may have noticed there's nothing to steal, except linder blocks too heavy for bandits to easily haul. And when they saw that every quarry man was twice their size and wielding mallets and pickaxes, it didn't take much to run them off the mountain. They won't return."

"I see," said Olana.

"We accept these terms and invite you to do the same," said Miri, waiting for Olana to respond. The silence poked at Miri's confidence, and she shifted her feet in the rock debris and tried not to squirm under the weight of Olana's hesitation. "Um, so do you?"

"Do I accept these *terms?*" Olana pulled long each vowel sound, an effect that had always made Miri cold for what she would do next. "I'll go ponder the matter, and I'll be sure to let you know."

Olana was turning away when Katar spoke.

"If forced to wait long, we're likely to return to the village. At that point you would have a long walk to make before telling us your decision. That will prove time lost on our studies, and if we're not presentable when the prince arrives, it will reflect badly on our tutor."

Miri frowned. She had forgotten *Assert a deadline for acceptance*.

A slow smile crept from one corner of Olana's mouth to the other. Some of the girls looked at one another, uneasy at what such a reaction could mean.

Then, unexpectedly, Olana applauded.

"I am impressed," said Olana. "I hadn't expected as much from mountain girls."

"We may be mountain girls," said Britta, "but we're also Danlanders."

"Indeed," said Olana. "This has been a very good

demonstration of Diplomacy. Let's return to our studies and see if we can't get you to the same level in every subject. Your terms are accepted." She entered the building.

Several of the girls exhaled at once, and the sound made them laugh.

"Olana might be a good sort after all," said Frid with some surprise.

"We had her by the hair," said Miri. "She had no choice."

Miri caught up with Katar on the academy steps. "I'm glad you spoke up or we could still be standing out here waiting."

Katar cut her eyes at Miri. "I'm a better diplomat than you and everyone knows it. It should've been me talking. Too bad for you that academy princess isn't based on who everyone likes best." She pinched Miri's arm and stomped up the steps.

Miri rubbed her arm and rolled her eyes at Britta.

"She is a sour one," said Britta.

Esa nodded. "And not worth the trouble. Katar's a thornbush protecting a hare that's too skinny to eat."

The morning after returning to the academy, Miri arose before the others, stretched, and leaned against

the window to watch the sun rise. The fade to day happened so gradually, Miri was surprised when she noticed it was light enough to see the stones littering the ground outside, rough with bites of morning frost. Only after the other girls were stirring and she was about to follow them to the dining hall did she look down.

On the outside of the windowsill was a piece of linder as long as her open hand, the kind streaked with pale pink veins. It was carved in the likeness of a hawk, sharp eyes, curved beak, wings outstretched. Miri now noticed footprints in the soft mud around the house leading up to the window, then turning and heading back toward the village until they disappeared into the rocks of the roadway.

She remembered how Peder had called her a hawk, always staring at the sky, at the mountain view, or out the window toward the village. She smiled to realize he guessed that she would be at the window, that she would see it first and know it was for her.

"I'm his best friend," she sang to the window, sang down into her toes, and out perhaps for the whole world to hear. For the moment, she did not care who knew the secret that made her chest tight and her head as light as seeding weeds in a breeze. *I'm his best friend.*

Chapter Fourteen

She's as lovely as a girl with flowers in her hair
The mountain, my lady
She's as bright as spring sun drying rain from the air
Mount Eskel, my lady

By a week following spring holiday, all traces of winter had vanished from the mountain. The last hard patches of snow melted into the mud, then the mud hardened and grasses grew. The miri flowers sprang up in the rock cracks, faced the sun, and twirled themselves in the breeze. On breaks, the girls spun the pink flowers and made wishes.

Miri found herself again on a hill, watching the last miri petal fall. She touched the linder hawk hidden in her pocket and thought of one wish she could make. Then she turned west, away from the village, toward the pass and the lowlands, and thought of a different wish.

She dropped the flower stem and laughed before she could even form the thought. Of course she did not wish to be the princess. How could she wish to marry someone she did not know? Katar's talk about being special and doing great things had lodged in her head, Miri decided, and she just needed to shake that nonsense loose.

But her eyes flicked back to the west. What wonders waited in the lowlands? There was, of course, that beautiful house for Pa and Marda, but whenever she thought of giving them that gift, she could not imagine herself actually wedded to a prince. For a moment she let herself wonder how such a future would change her.

"Princess Miri," she whispered, and surprised herself by feeling a thrill. The title added weight to her name, made her feel more significant. Miri was a scrawny, hopeless village girl, but who would Princess Miri be?

Other girls on the hill watched the last petal on their miri flowers tick off and float away. Miri wondered how many were wishing to wear a silver gown and how many were wishing for a title before their name.

"I used to think that was the whole world," said Esa, sitting beside Miri with Britta and Frid. Esa's eyes sought out the swells and slopes of the mountains dimming from green to gray on the northern horizon.

"Now I feel so small, perched up here on our isolated mountain."

Miri nodded. That morning a lecture from Olana had shaken a dreary spirit over their heads—linder represented a tiny fraction of the Danlander economy, less than the sale of pig ears or cloth flowers for ladies' hats; the entire population of Mount Eskel was smaller than the number of palace stable hands; the wooden chapel doors, so loved and prized by the village, were smaller and less ornate than the front doors of any Aslandian merchant.

"The lowlands aren't so different from here," said Britta. "Just bigger and . . ."

"*A lot* bigger," said Frid.

"It's hard to feel like I matter at all," said Esa.

Katar strolled by, twirling a bare miri stem. "A princess matters."

When no one argued, Miri knew she had not been the only one contemplating the western horizon when making her wish. The world had never felt so wide, a great gaping mouth that could swallow all of them whole. It made Miri wish she could bite back.

"It doesn't seem to matter what we think," said Miri. "The prince will come up here and look at us as if we're barrels in a trader's wagon. And if I'm salt pork and he doesn't care for salt pork, then there's nothing I can do."

Her eyes found Katar walking down the hill. *But I can do something about academy princess*, she thought.

It would be harder than she had hoped. The older girls had been spooked by Miri's tie with Katar after the first exam, and Bena, Katar, and Liana spent all their free time with open books. Miri gazed longingly at spring erupting outside the window but forced herself to study—at least, most of the time. Britta, Esa, and Frid could coax her outside for a nostalgic game of Wolf and Rabbit every so often.

At first, the new arrangement with Olana felt little better than before. She was tense and short of temper, as if uneasy with the threat of tutoring ruffians in a swamp but unable to soften her hard demeanor. But gradually Miri felt the mood ease. The girls who at first tried to take advantage of the new situation found after a lost meal that they should still listen to Olana.

Just before the arrival of the traders would afford them a week off, Olana held another exam and announced the top five scores. Katar was first and Miri second.

"Sorry, Miri," said Katar. "You know you're too short to look right in that gown, anyway."

"You're too tall to . . . ," Miri stumbled, unable to think of a good response. She cursed herself silently. "Never mind."

Esa was shocked and thrilled to hear she was third, until Bena and Liana caught up to her on their walk home for the next rest day.

"I think you girls on the fourteen-year-olds' row are cheating," said Bena.

"I wasn't cheating, Bena," said Esa. "I've been studying."

"Oh? So have I, and there's no chance both you and Miri could beat me. I'll be watching you."

"Me too," said Liana.

"I guess they don't like anyone who is competition," said Miri after the older girls had moved away.

"At least I *am* competition," Esa said cheerfully.

The girls were a few minutes from the village when the sound of a donkey bawling echoed off the mountainside. A caravan of trader wagons came up from behind, Enrik at the lead.

"Britta, they're here," Miri whispered, pressing a hand to her belly. "What if it doesn't work? What if they refuse to trade for gold, take away the supplies, and we can't get the linder down to a market, and—"

"The academy released you all for the trading, did they?" said Enrik, squinting at the girls as he rode by. "Well, I hope your people have been hard at work without you. I should be grumpy to come all the way here for half a load of linder."

Miri and the girls ran behind the wagons and reached the village a few minutes after them. The traders were stopped before a gathering of villagers. Os stood at their head.

"This is outrageous!" one of the traders was saying. "We won't buy your linder at such prices. Then what will you do? Starve, that's what."

"That's a risk we take," said Os. A brief glance at Miri's father was the only sign that he might be unsure. Pa folded his arms, a stance that made him appear twice as broad and as solid as the mountain.

"If you refuse," Os continued, "we'll manage to haul our linder down the mountain ourselves, sell it at the first town for triple what you pay, and make the local merchants there rich when they resell the stone to the capital for triple what they paid. We'll win, they'll win, everyone will win. Except you."

The pause that followed made Miri want to hop from foot to foot. If it worked, their lives would change. If not, if Miri's suggestion ruined everything . . . She shut her eyes, afraid to think about it.

"Do you think they'll agree?" Britta whispered.

"I don't know," said Miri, curling and extending her toes inside her boots. "But I wish they'd hurry and decide, whatever they do."

"When we get back to Asland and the king hears

about this," said a trader with white hair and a smooth face, "he'll send others to mine the linder. I've half a mind to do it myself."

"Go right ahead," said Os, his arm open and gesturing to the quarry.

The trader hesitated, and many of the lowlanders exchanged glances.

"Do you have any idea what it takes to find quiet stone?" said Doter in her round, loud voice. "Quiet stone—the linder that sleeps, that is good and sound, has fissures in just the right places, but not too many. Do you have the ear to hear where to break it from the mountain, the eye to know where to slide the wedge, how many taps of the mallet, not one too many, not one too few? And then there's the squaring to be done. You're fools, the lot of you, if you think we're not aware that we're the only people alive who know this mountain and know linder and how to harvest it for palaces and kings. So don't try that threat on us again."

A gush of warmth entered Miri's chest, she felt so proud and happy to be part of a people who knew a craft no one else did. She wanted to run to Esa's mother and hug her, and the desire pricked in her heart the old, tiny wound that reminded her she did not have a mother of her own. She sidled up to her pa.

After Doter's lecture, both sides were quiet,

waiting for a decision. Miri wondered if worry could actually kill a person.

Enrik moaned, running a hand through his greasy hair. "I told you there was a risk all that learning at the academy might smarten them up, and now it's come to this." He turned to Os. "Fine, but your asking price is too high to account for our costs and reasonable profit. I'll give you one gold piece for three blocks of linder."

Miri had to sit down, she was so dizzy with relief.

"Enrik!" one of the traders shouted.

"I'm not going back empty-handed," said Enrik.

Soon others were agreeing as well, some less reluctant than others, and trading began. Many villagers came to Miri to verify fair prices. Miri said, "Yes, I think so," or, "I'd ask for a bit more." For the moment, in her woolens and braided hair, she felt as important as she imagined she would in the silver gown and a crown.

Since the traders had not hauled enough supplies to trade for the linder at the new prices, they purchased the surplus with gold and silver coins. Os asked Britta to make sure they were genuine, and Britta examined each one, hefted it in her palm, bit down, and nodded approval.

Half the village put their shoulders to loading the

finished blocks in the wagons. As the traders and villagers worked together, Miri was surprised to hear pleasant chatter. Some even agreed to stay the evening and share a meal with the villagers.

Miri stood by her sister, observing a trader pat a quarrier on the back. "Seems strange. I thought they'd dislike us even more."

"Maybe it's hard to respect someone you're cheating," said Marda.

When the work outside the quarry slowed, Miri took Britta's hand and they walked through the village, Miri recounting who had married whose son, recent quarry injuries, family secrets, and any other village tidbits she could think of to help Britta feel more at home.

Just when Miri was enacting an exuberant retelling of the time Frid's brother was so woozy after a spinning dance that he fell face first into goat droppings, Peder walked by. He did not so much as glance at Miri, as though she were a stranger, as though their conversation at spring holiday and the linder hawk on the windowsill had been daydreams. She stared, stunned by a twinge in her chest. She hated the feeling and needed a laugh to dislodge it.

"Britta, did I tell you about when Peder decided to take a winter bath?"

Peder stopped when he heard his name. Miri kept talking without looking his way.

"He had stolen my straw doll, and I was chasing him out past the chapel. It'd been sunny the day before and melted snow filled up the old quarry holes, so you couldn't tell flat ground from the pits. He'd just turned around to taunt me when, *whoosh!*" Miri mimed Peder dropping down. "He disappeared completely. You should've seen the surprise on his face when his head popped back up, like he thought the whole world had been tugged out from under his feet. He climbed out, soaked, his hair straight and hanging down in his face, and he said in this shocked, breathless voice, 'What'd you do?'"

Britta was laughing, and she snorted, turned red, and laughed harder.

Peder grinned. "I still think you did something."

"Yes, that's right. I dug a hole, filled it with icy water, tempted you into stealing my doll, and forced you to run directly into it. . . ."

"I wouldn't put it past her," Peder said to Britta.

"The doll was ruined, but it was worth it to see that surprise frozen on his face."

"You laugh now," said Peder, "but best take care what your flapping mouth reveals or I might have to tell how one spring holiday you threw off all your clothes and ran out—"

Miri put her hand over Peder's mouth. "I was three," she said through her laughs. "Three years old. Three!"

Peder's eyes widened impishly, and he laughed under her hand. She thought of trying to wrestle him to the ground, then realized that she was touching him and he had not pushed her away. Her old fear seized her, and she let him go.

"Peder!" his father called, and he ran off to help in the quarry. Miri put her hand in her pocket and held the linder hawk.

"You like him, don't you?" asked Britta when he was too far away to hear.

Miri shrugged. "Do you?"

"I don't think any of the boys in the village know I'm here."

"Oh, yes? Then what about Jans?"

"Do you know that you avoid talking about Peder?" Britta asked.

"Or maybe you just avoid talking about Jans."

"Miri," said Britta with a touch of exasperation.

Miri slumped onto a boulder. "What should I say? That I like him so much it hurts?"

"Maybe you should tell him."

"But what if I do and he looks at me like I'm salt

fish rotten in the barrel, and then I can never be his friend again?"

Miri waited for Britta to say something reassuring, but she just nodded.

"Never mind, I'm not really worried about it," Miri said quickly, trying to affect indifference. "I guess I shouldn't keep you to myself when you haven't been home yet."

"Honestly," said Britta, "the academy feels more like home to me than my second cousin's house."

"Aren't they kind to you?"

"They're not unkind," said Britta. "When I arrived, I brought food and supplies so I wouldn't be a burden, but I still feel, I don't know, not unwelcome, just unwanted."

"Do you miss your real parents?"

"No," said Britta. "Does that make me a bad person? I miss other people from the lowlands—a woman who used to take care of me, a family that lived nearby. But my father was always gone, and my mother was . . ." She shrugged, unable to finish her sentence. She stared hard at the ground with eyes wide open, as if trying to dry them out.

Miri did not want Britta to cry and so changed the subject. "Would you like to spend this week at our house? You can share my pallet."

Britta nodded. "I'd like that."

"Then so would I, Lady Britta."

They had reached Britta's house, so Britta stepped in to greet her relatives, and Miri continued on to the quarry.

From the near edge, she could see the green stream come down the high slope, jog around the quarry pit, and then empty below it, now milk white. The air was powdered with fine, white dust. The half-exposed slabs and laboring villagers gave the place energy, a feeling that here was where all the work of the world was done. Here everything was important.

Sometimes just looking at it made Miri's chest feel hollow.

Her father was loading a block onto a trader wagon. He saw her, brushed his hands clean, and put his arm around her shoulder. Miri thought the gesture meant he was proud of how she had helped with the trading, or she hoped it did. *At least I have that much to offer the village,* she thought. She turned to him and took in the father-smell of his shirt.

Her father's arm tensed, and she looked to where he was staring.

Two boys were pulling a block up the steep slope of the quarry pit, and Marda was behind them. She acted as a stone braker, inserting two wooden wedges beneath the stone every few paces to prevent it from falling back in case the rope slipped. Miri was small, but stone braking did not take great strength. She had always believed she could be the best stone braker in the quarry, if given the chance.

Pa did not take his eyes off Marda. "I don't like it," was all he said. He let his arm drop from Miri's shoulder and started toward the quarry.

Miri heard the silent boom of a common quarry-speech warning—*Watch out*, said one of the boys pulling the block. The other boy had let the rope rub against the corner of the stone. It was fraying.

"Marda!" Pa was running now. Marda did not turn out of the way. She was still trying to lodge a wedge under the stone. As the boys scrambled for the rope, it snapped, and Marda disappeared from view.

Miri scrambled over the lip and inside the quarry for the first time in her life. Halfway down the slope Marda lay on her side, her face white with pain, strips of cloth ripped off her legging. Pa cradled her head in his lap.

"Marda, are you all right?" Miri knelt beside her in the rock debris, while other workers rushed in. "What can I—"

"Get out," said her pa. His face was red, and anger filled out his voice and built it loud. She had never heard him speak much above a whisper.

"But I . . . but—"

"Get out!"

Miri found herself stumbling and running backward even before she could swallow her shock, turn, and flee. She left the quarry and did not stop and thought to just keep running until she fell. But someone stopped her. It was Doter, Peder's ma.

"Let me go," said Miri, kicking and thrashing. Until she spoke, she had not realized that she was sobbing.

"Come here. Hush now, come on." Doter held her tighter and tighter until Miri stopped struggling. She laid her head on the big woman's shoulder and let herself cry.

"There you go," said Doter, "let it all slide out. Unhappiness can't stick in a person's soul when it's slick with tears."

"Marda . . . was in an . . . in an accident," said Miri through the sobs.

"I saw. She's got a hurt leg, but I think she'll be all right. Take a moment and make sure you are, little flower."

"Why does he throw me out all the time?" Miri's throat was sore from sobbing. She pounded her fist against her knee, angry and embarrassed to be crying in front of someone, hating how it made her feel like a helpless little girl. "Am I so small and stupid and useless?"

"Don't you know?" Doter sighed, and her chest heaved beneath Miri's head. "Oh, my Miri flower, why do you think he keeps you out of the quarry?"

"Because he's ashamed," said Miri with years of bitterness rushing in her blood. "Because I'm too scrawny to do any good."

"Laren, you big, dumb, tight-lipped fool," said Doter to herself. "I should've known better, I should've known he was too much of a *man* to explain. Everyone in the world knows but the girl, the only one who should. Shame on you, Doter, for not speaking up years ago. . . ."

Miri felt stilled and soothed by Doter's talk. She wrestled with her sobs until they were subdued to quiet, painful shakes in her chest. It was useless to interrupt when Doter conversed with herself, though Miri was hungry to hear whatever secret was behind it.

At last Doter sighed. "Miri, do you know how your ma died?"

"She was sick after she had me."

Miri felt Doter nod. "That's true, but there's more to tell. It was high summer and traders were coming up any day. There'd been a costly number of accidents that year, and the quarry didn't have enough cut stone to trade for the next month's supplies. Your ma, she was a stubborn girl, and though big as a full moon with you in her belly, she insisted on helping out in the quarry. You may be able to guess what happened."

"She was stone braking," Miri said softly.

"One of the boys tripped, the stone slipped, and your ma tumbled down the steep side. That night you were born before your time. She hung on for a week, but she'd bled a lot, and there are some things a person can't survive."

"For that week, she didn't let me out of her arms."

"Of course not, why would she? You were tiny and scrawny and fuzzy, and also the most beautiful baby I've ever seen, excepting my own."

Miri started to protest, but she never could argue with Doter. Os often said, *A wise one never doubts the words from Doter's mouth.*

Doter grasped Miri's shoulders and held her at arm's length. Miri let her hair fall forward to hide any signs of crying, but Doter had a round, glad face and just looking at her made Miri feel easier.

"No one cares that you don't work in the quarry," said Doter. Miri choked on this and struggled to free herself, but Doter pinched her shoulders harder, as if determined to be heard. "I'm telling you now, no one cares. Do you think anyone begrudges my girl Esa her time tending house? When Laren says, Miri won't work in this quarry, everyone nods and never speaks another word about it. You believe me, don't you?"

Miri shuddered, a last sob breaking loose.

"Your pa is a house with shutters closed," said Doter. "There are things going on inside that a person can't see, but you sense he has a wound that won't heal."

Miri nodded.

"Marda takes after your pa, but you, Miri, you are your ma alive again. Look at your blue eyes, your hair like a hawk feather. He can't help seeing you and thinking of her. It nearly killed Laren to let Marda work in the quarry, but he had no choice with just three of you in the house. How could he bear letting his little girl step foot into the place that took the life of her ma?"

They walked back through the village, and Miri kept her eyes on the ground before her. The whole world had shifted, and she was not sure she could keep her feet.

She was her ma alive again.

When Miri returned, she found Marda moved from the quarry into their house. Frid's mother had pronounced the injury a painful leg break but nothing serious. While the woman set the broken leg, Miri held Marda's hand, kissed her cheek, plaited her hair, and loved her as much as she felt, as much as she imagined her mother would. That night, Miri gave Britta her pallet and slept curled up beside her sister to comb her hair or stroke her face when Marda could not sleep for the pain.

Early the next morning, Miri woke to see her pa sitting in a chair, staring at his hands. She rose and padded to him, her bare feet silent. He reached out for her without looking up and pulled her into his chest.

"I'm sorry, my flower."

He held her tighter, and when his breath shook on a sob, Miri did not need to hear any more words.

He was sorry. She was his flower. They would be all right.

Chapter Fifteen

Look no farther than your hand
Make a choice and take a stand

In a mountain summer, the world savored each day. Dawn came early, inviting waking up slowly and stretching and looking forward to everything. Olana noticed the class's attention straying to the window, so she held more and more class time out of doors. The girls spent weeks learning the dances for the ball, twirling, skipping, and sliding under the sun. The hard blue of the sky appeared to arch above their heads a mere arm's length away. Sometimes Miri reached and jumped and fancied she nearly brushed its smooth, curved shell.

Miri had never felt like this, light enough to float into the clouds. Even Katar's jabs and Bena's and Liana's turned backs did not hurt so much—Doter's story draped around her. What she had long believed was not true, and now the world was wide open to discover what was.

One evening after chores, Miri sat with Britta, Esa, and Frid on her pallet in the corner of the bedchamber and confided in them the story of her mother.

"So, did you . . . do you think I'm a burden on the village?" Miri spoke low enough that her voice would not carry. She did not want to give Katar anything else to taunt her about. "That I'm too weak to work in the quarry?"

Frid frowned. "No one on Mount Eskel is too weak to work in the quarry. I heard my ma say once that your pa kept you home for his own reasons. I guess I never thought about it again."

Miri rubbed her arms and laughed. "It's wonderful, it's just so hard to believe. It's like all my life I thought the sky was green."

Esa lay on her stomach, one arm propping up her chin. "The way you act, always laughing out loud, saying what you think, I never would've guessed you worried what anyone thought."

Britta had a shrewd smile. "I keep thinking about a tale my nurse used to read to me about a bird whose wings are pinned to the ground. Have you heard it? In the end, when he finally frees himself, he flies so high he becomes a star. My nurse said the story was about how we all have something that keeps us down. So here's what I'm wondering—if Miri's wings are free, what will she do now?"

Esa grinned. "Fly away, Miri bird, fly away!"

Miri flapped her arms and cawed.

"What *are* you doing?" said Bena, annoyed.

The girls laughed.

Where should I fly? Miri asked herself all summer as she traveled between the academy and home.

Olana did not like it, but she lived by the agreement and allowed the girls a week off with each trader visit. Word of a village with gold coins to spend must have reached many ears, and traders new to the mountain arrived with specialty goods like strong-soled shoes, dyed cloth, chairs that rocked, ceramic cups, metal pails, painted ribbons, and steel needles. The village's food stores built up, so no one had to wait with empty barrels for the next trader visit.

At midsummer, Marda and Pa presented Miri with a new pair of boots for her fifteenth birthday. She marveled how she could not feel the sharper stones through the soles.

Marda was resting while her leg healed, so each day at home, Miri helped her sister to the shade of an evergreen tree beside their house and with a shard of rubble rock scratched letters on the old quarry wall. On later visits she brought a book filched from Olana's shelf, and the day came when Marda read an entire page on her own. She leaned back her head and sighed.

"What's the matter?" asked Miri.

"Nothing. It feels good." She looked to where the sun was grazing the western hills. "You know how the lowlanders have always been with us, how the traders talk and such. I've wondered if they were right, if we aren't as smart, if there's something wrong with us. With me."

"Marda! How could you believe them?"

"How could I not? When you first started to teach me, I was terrified. You've done so well, and I was sure I'd be too dull to learn. The whole village would be thinking how Miri's the head of the academy but her sister's got goat brains."

"No one could think that, especially not now that you're the only one outside the academy who can read. Besides, Katar's first in the class."

Marda raised her brows. "But if you want to be, I don't know of anything that could stop you."

Miri almost told Marda then of feeling like the outcast of the quarry and the mean, tight spot of jealousy she had harbored in her heart for years. But the sensation was loosening, and it did not seem to matter as much anymore.

Before the academy, she had sat on her hill watching

goats, and her imagination could dream of nothing grander than working in the quarry. But now she was aware of the kingdom beyond her mountain, hundreds of years of history, and a thousand things she could be.

She would not test her father's pain and ask to work in the quarry again. She would find her own place. And sitting under a tree with Marda as she read her first page felt like the best place in the entire world. Miri wondered how she could make that good feeling last.

Chapter Sixteen

I cut all day and I squared all night
And I thought I'd mined the mountain's might
Then I saw all my work by the bright dawn light
The mountain was the world and my labor a mite

One early morning at the academy, Miri went outside before breakfast to stretch and look out over the mountains. A wind came out of the north and whipped the end of her shirt tight against her hips. It smelled far away, not familiar and warm like summer wind, but of empty places, trees Miri did not know, and snow. The scent made her muscles tense. It meant summer was over, autumn was dawning, and the ball was just weeks away.

In the academy, the mood changed with the weather. Every day that passed was one day less to learn how to impress the prince and not look like an utter fool. The dances were practiced with uptight clumsiness, the curtsies with anxious stumbles. Olana yelled at them, "Do you want to look like imbeciles?

Do you really want the guests to believe every frightful thing they've heard about the outlying territories? Stand up straighter, pronounce your words. For pity's sake, stop looking like you want to humiliate me!"

Miri tried to remember when every curtsy had begun to feel more important than breakfast.

For some of the summer, Miri had spent outdoor breaks teaching Britta quarry songs and running over the hills. Now change pulsed around them, and she felt pulled inside to bend over books and recite lists of kings and queens. Soon most of the other girls were studying through breaks and rest days as well. She found herself glancing often at Katar, wondering if the older girl had caught things that Miri missed, or staring at the painting of the house with hope so strong that it felt like something she could reach out and grab. When she found herself in such a mood, she tried not to think of Peder at all. Her mind and heart tangled.

Then Olana announced the final exam. Each girl read aloud from a book and was judged on pronunciation and clarity. Knut stood in for the prince, and the girls toe-heeled across the room and curtsied to him. He never put down his stirring spoon and met each girl's eyes as if it pained him terribly, but with Miri he managed a half smile.

During Miri's turn at Dance, Katar caught her eye

and winked. Miri staggered in the midst of a step, looked away, and tried to concentrate.

"It's all right, Miri," said Britta, who was acting as her dance partner. "You're doing really well."

Miri could hear Bena whisper her name.

After the individual tests, the girls followed Olana to the top of a slope where the ground was softened with grass. The wind from the valley smelled as fresh as wind-dried laundry, and the sun warmed the top of Miri's head as though giving her a pat. She leaned back on her hands and felt her shoulders relax for the first time in a week. She was confident that she would pass.

"Take a long look," said Olana, gesturing to the northern horizon. "It's the only view some of you will ever see. So far, several have not done well enough to pass the exam and attend the ball. Now is your last chance to redeem yourselves. Those who are near to failing must answer correctly each question or you will remain hidden in the bedchamber while everyone else dances and makes eyes at the prince."

Olana sat the girls in a circle and began the decisive quiz. Miri recounted the first five kings of Danland beginning with King Dan and Katar supplied the next five. Frid stumbled with her question but came up with a correct answer.

Then Olana turned to Gerti. "Name the years of the War of Rights."

Gerti's faced drained of color. She squinted at the sky, her eyes searching, but hopelessness made lines on her brow. Miri watched Gerti's struggle and amazed herself by feeling relieved. In the contest for academy princess, everyone was competition.

"The answer, Gerti," said Olana.

"I . . ."

Miri thought of the painting of the house, of Marda saying that nothing could get in Miri's way, of the silver gown with tiny rosebuds and the feeling that buzzed in her bones when she thought of the significance the title "Princess" would add to her name. At that moment, it all felt wispy and weedy compared with Gerti's immediate need.

It's just not fair, Miri thought. *Everyone has studied hard all year. We should at least get the chance to go to the ball.*

Her decision seemed obvious. She would try to help.

Her instinct was to use quarry-speech. *But how can I tell Gerti a number of a year?* She had found a way to tell the girls to run. If she could find the right thought, she might be able to communicate anything, particularly as the academy girls had so many shared memories. It could work. It just might.

By her foot, a single miri flower wiggled in the breeze. That gave her hope. The pink flowers seemed to thrive around beds of linder. The entire area had once been a working quarry, and surely there was a remnant. Still, Miri had heard it work only with solid stone like the living quarry and the floor of the academy.

Olana sighed. "Just say you don't know, Gerti, and we'll move on."

Gerti's lip quivered. Miri sank her hand into the autumn grass. There must be linder deep down. She pushed harder and hoped.

Despite what Peder had said, she still liked to sing aloud when quarry-speaking; it helped her focus the internal singing that pushed her memory into the stone. But she could not risk it here. She pressed the ground and thought of her favorite block-squaring chant: "The mountain was the world and my labor was a mite." She organized her thoughts and sang them silently in the rhythm of that chant.

Miri recalled the History lesson when Olana first had talked about the War of Rights. A fly had been caught in the room, buzzing madly and thumping the window. Miri remembered because she had wondered how many times that crazy fly could bounce off the glass before knocking itself unconscious, and she had decided 212 times, the first year of the war.

"Two hundred twelve to two hundred seventy-six," Olana had said. "Say it, class."

Thump, thump, went the fly.

"Two hundred twelve to two hundred seventy-six," they had repeated.

Thump, thump, thump-thump.

Miri sang the memory into the earth—the fly drumming on the window, Olana declaring the years, the class repeating. Perhaps Gerti had noticed the fly, too. Perhaps with that nudge, the memory would come forward for her and the sound of those years fall from her mind to her tongue. Miri's vision shivered, her thoughts clicked, that moment painted itself in full color in her mind, but Gerti's face did not change. Miri tried again, her quarry-speech song roaring inside her.

"If you haven't remembered by now, Gerti, you won't," said Olana. "Now then, Liana, please name—"

"Two hundred and . . ." Gerti looked up. She appeared to be trying to taste something peculiar or identify a distant smell. "Two hundred and twelve to two hundred and, uh, seventy. Seventy-six, I mean, seventy-six."

Katar elbowed Miri in the ribs, having no doubt detected Miri's quarry-speech as well. Miri smiled back pleasantly.

"Hm. That's correct," said Olana.

Gerti looked at Miri and smiled as big as the sky. Olana returned to Liana, who answered correctly, as did the next girl. Then Tonna tripped up over the first rule of Conversation.

Miri had not thought of continuing her silent hints, but she believed Tonna had as much right to attend the ball as Gerti. A jab from Katar and a warning look decided her. Miri searched for the perfect memory and sang it down into the mountain's hidden linder and up into the minds of any listeners. Tonna sighed relief and answered the question.

Miri smiled. It was beginning to be fun.

The exam continued while the sun arced west, dragging their shadows longer. Whenever a girl faltered or looked Miri's way, she did her best to communicate a helpful memory. She was relieved that Britta always knew her answers.

Then Frid could not remember the last rule of diplomatic negotiations. Miri quarry-spoke of the day Olana had introduced the rules of Diplomacy, but Frid just stared at the ground with her familiar wide-eyed expression and seemed resolved to defeat. Miri dug her fingers deeper into the earth, and if she had sung aloud, her quarry-speech would have been a shout;

but no recognition crossed Frid's face. Whether the memory was unclear or the quarry-speech was too faint on that hill, it was not working.

"I'm sorry," Miri whispered.

"Silence," warned Olana.

Then another voice in quarry-speech, faint, delicate. The feeling of that voice could not have been more clearly Gerti's than if she had spoken aloud. Miri closed her eyes to concentrate and saw in her mind her negotiations with Olana when she had forgotten the final rule and Katar had stepped in.

Frid's dull eyes sparkled. "Give them a limit for accepting the terms."

"'Assert a deadline for acceptance' is the correct answer," said Olana, "but that will do."

Gerti beamed.

And from then on, no one hesitated on an answer without being deluged with hints from a dozen different girls, some less helpful, some exact, but the flailing girl always managed to sort through them and come up with the correct answer. On the outside, the girls were serene but for a few sly smiles, their hands resting casually on the ground as if interested in the grass. But on the inside, the feeling of that quarry-speech was like ten songs sung at once, all in different voices, all joyous.

So anxious were the girls to help, Miri did not have another chance to step in, save once.

"Did you hear me, Katar?" said Olana. "What is the formal name of the curtsy used only for a king on his throne?"

"I, uh . . ."

Katar looked at the sky, at the ground, at her fingernails, anywhere but at the girls, as if refusing to ask for help. And no one offered. Miri thought it possible that none of the girls could recall, but many placed their hands in their laps, explicit in their refusal. Even Bena and Liana looked over their shoulders and examined the aspect of the far hill. Katar's glance flicked to Miri for the briefest moment, and then away.

To Miri's recollection, Olana had given the name of the curtsy only once, but Miri had read it recently during personal study. Katar would pass the exam without her help, but she might not score high enough to be academy princess. Miri grappled with herself. She did not want to give Katar anything, but her sense of justice would not allow her to help every girl but one. Miri glared at Katar, slapped her hand on the grass, and sang mutely of Olana's introductory lecture on Poise. After a few moments, Katar nodded. Her voice was very quiet.

"I remember now." She cleared her throat. "It's called the heart's offering."

After the last question, Olana whistled a long note of approval.

"You all scored one hundred percent on this portion of the exam. I didn't expect that. Well, go on to dinner, and I'll calculate the scores for the entire exam. After dinner, I'll announce who passed and who will be academy princess."

Little food was consumed that evening. Miri watched the fat congeal in her egg-and-wheat-bread soup and listened to the whispered conversations of the other girls. Knut passed behind her and muttered, "This is the last time I bother to cook something nice on a test day."

"You cooked something nice?" said Miri. "Where is it?"

Knut tousled her hair.

Katar pushed away her full bowl and stared out the window. Miri realized that both girls' legs were shaking, their knees banging the bottom of the table.

"Looks like Katar and I are doing our best to harvest and square this table before the traders come," said Miri, and several girls laughed.

Miri had joked to break the tension and now braced herself for the inevitable retort, but Katar just stood and left. Miri rested her chin in her hands, happy to have the better of Katar for once.

"It's time," Olana called.

The classroom chairs squeaked as the girls sat and adjusted themselves. Miri thought she might not be the only one holding her breath. Olana held a parchment. Her eyes seemed pleased, though her mouth gave no hint of a smile.

"Due to the unexpected performance on the final test, you all passed," she said.

A squeal of delight went up. Olana read the parchment with the order of the scores, starting with the lowest. Most of the girls at the bottom of the list did not seem to mind their place and were pleased to hear that they would be going to the ball at all. Olana stopped reading before Miri heard her own name.

"The last five girls—Katar, Esa, Liana, Bena, and Miri—were so close, I could not determine the leader. So I will allow you to decide."

Katar's shoulders slumped. Miri felt her leg shaking again as her classmates whispered their votes to Olana one by one. When the last girl sat down, Olana smiled.

"Over half of you voted for the same girl, a clear majority. Miri, come forward."

Miri's head was light, and as she walked to the

front of the class she seemed to float, as though she were a puff of tree pollen blown just above the ground. She kept her eyes on Britta, who was grinning madly.

Olana put her hand on Miri's shoulder. "The academy princess."

And the girls cheered.

After they were dismissed for bed, Miri stepped outside to have a moment with the sunset, gold and orange that pulled the sky close. She needed a break from a teary Liana consoling a red-faced Bena and the scalding stares of some very jealous seventeen- and eighteen-year-olds. It had been quite clear who had not voted for Miri.

From a spot at the cliff's edge, Miri could see the mountains and hills ringing out from Mount Eskel like water ripples from a thrown stone. Just below her, instead of sheer cliff, a shelf stuck out, so if she happened to slip on rubble rock, she would land on the ledge instead of falling a long way down. She saw now that this spot was not only *her* favorite; Katar sat on the rocky outcrop, her knees pulled into her chest.

Miri climbed down and tried to think of something really good to say. She was just about to open her mouth when Katar made a sound like a strained hiccup.

It couldn't be a sob, thought Miri. She had never seen Katar cry. But when Katar turned toward the light, there was an unmistakable sheen of tears.

"Go ahead and gloat," said Katar.

Miri frowned. She thought Katar was acting like a baby to cry just because she did not win.

"Go on," said Katar. "Say how you're going to wear that gown and dance first and be beautiful and go to Asland to be the future queen."

"That's not true, Katar. Just because I'm academy princess doesn't mean he'll choose me."

"Yes, he will."

Would he really? "I have a chance, but—"

"It was my *only* chance. Nobody really likes me, so how will he?"

"Do you want to marry him so much?" asked Miri.

"I don't care about the prince," Katar snapped back. "I just wanted a way to leave here. I hate it here." Her voice went soft, as if the words were almost too strong to speak aloud.

Katar tossed a piece of rubble rock, and Miri heard it strike the slope below, disturbing other stones as it rolled. She was waiting for Katar to amend her statement, but she did not.

After a few moments, Miri said, "You don't really *hate* it here."

"Yes, I do. Why wouldn't I?" Katar hurled another stone over the edge. When she spoke again, her voice shook. "I know I'm not liked. I can't help how I am, but I feel so tired never having anywhere to go where I feel good. Not at home, certainly, not with my ma dead."

"My mother died, too," said Miri.

"But your pa adores you. I've seen him look at you and Marda as if you were the mountain itself, as if you were the world."

He does? thought Miri. Her heart beat once as she thought, *He does.*

"My father doesn't look at me at all," said Katar. "Maybe he blames me for my mother dying when I was born, or maybe he just wishes I were a boy or some other girl entirely. Everything about this place is cold and hard and sharp and mean and . . . and I just want to go away. I want to be somebody else and see other things. And now I never will."

Miri shivered at a breeze coming up from the valley. All her life she had seen herself as the only lonesome thing in the world, but now even Katar seemed but a small child lost on a far hill.

Katar held her face in her hands and sobbed, and Miri patted her shoulder awkwardly.

"I'm sorry," Miri said.

Katar shrugged, and Miri knew there was nothing she could say. A true friend might have been able to comfort Katar, but Miri felt she barely knew the girl beside her.

Everything was strange and wonderful and wrong at once. The girls had chosen Miri as academy princess. Autumn thrummed fresh and cold on her skin. Any day the prince would come and take one of them away. And Katar sobbed misery at her side.

"I'm sorry," Miri said again, hating how hollow those words sounded. Katar had given her a small gift by opening her heart and showing her pain. Miri tucked the moment in her own heart and hoped somehow to repay.

Chapter Seventeen

Though the river is milk
It stops dead in my throat
Like a stone, stone, stone

After the exam, the girls were free to make their own schedules. Many passed the daylight hours practicing Conversation or Poise and rehearsing the dances, aware that the real test, the ball itself, was still to come. Others were relieved to have a break and lay around gossiping about the dresses the lowlanders would bring or roamed the mountainside to laugh, fret, and wonder.

The girls seemed to avoid the prickly topic of the prince and his choice of bride, but an uncertain excitement persisted in the academy. Even practical-minded Frid was prone to stare at the sky with a hint of a sheepish smile.

Miri wished Peder would come and remind her that she did not want to be chosen, but whenever she thought about the prince, a ticklish sensation filled her chest. She had let loose her dream of being a quarrier, but her heart still longed for something to hope for. Even though she now understood the reasons behind her exclusion from the quarry, when she imagined returning to the village just to tend goats, she felt a racing kind of panic. Surely there was some other place for her, something she could do to continue to stretch and grow, to be of use. To make her pa proud. The idea of being a princess promised many things.

One morning, Miri found Esa on the steps of the academy facing the mountain pass.

"It feels like any moment they'll come," said Miri, sitting beside her. "When I look that way and see a bird or a cloud's shadow sliding by, I think it's the first wagon, and my stomach about drops out of my middle."

Esa nodded, and Miri noticed that her eyes were sad.

"What's wrong?"

Esa shook her head as if dismissing Miri's concern. "The dancing."

"What do you mean? You passed the dancing exam just fine."

Esa looked up as if she had lost patience with herself. "I keep imagining the moment when I first dance with the prince, and he'll put out his arms, and I'll put my right hand in his, and he'll stare at my left arm and wonder why I don't move it, and then, when he understands, I picture how his face will change. . . ."

Esa breathed out long and slow. The sigh made Miri uneasy, and she wanted to get Esa to laugh.

"Maybe the prince will have an injured arm, too."

Esa snorted.

"No, really. Or maybe a lazy eye that will roll around in his head so he can look two places at once. You could pretend to be two different people and hop back and forth between his gazes, having a chat with yourself. Just don't forget to follow the rules of Conversation and continually bring the topic back around to, uh, to you."

Motion in Miri's periphery tugged her attention. It was no cloud shadow. Rock dust lifted around the first wagon as though it rode on drifting fog. Another followed. And another. The sheer number of wagons was thrilling and frightening. Some of the girls began to screech and run around, looking for either a place to better watch the arrival or a place to hide. Frid and Britta came to stand beside Miri and Esa.

"So many people," said Frid.

Britta seemed to hold her breath, and Miri thought how, despite all her assurances that she would not be chosen, Britta was as anxious as any of them.

Behind the initial wagons and mounted soldiers rolled a closed carriage, its window curtain drawn. It was made from pale wood the color of Esa's hair and pulled by four horses of the same shade. Miri stared at the window. Could the prince see her? The curtain shivered as if a hand touched it from behind. Certain that he was peering out, Miri smiled and gave a cheeky wave.

Esa giggled and slapped Miri's side with the back of her hand. "What are you doing? He might be looking."

"I hope he is," said Miri, though she did not wave again.

Olana rushed outside, ordering the girls out of the way and into their bedchamber. Through the window they watched the visitors set up tents, care for the horses, and unload barrels and boxes into the far side of the building. Whenever one of the girls went to use the outhouse, she reported smoke pouring out of all three kitchen chimneys.

"Did anyone see him?" asked Gerti, standing on her toes to get a better view out the window.

"I thought I did, for a second," said Helta, a thirteen-year-old with a snub nose and freckles. "He was tall and younger than I'd imagined and had dark hair."

The chatter in the room died away. The prince had suddenly become a real person with a height and an age and hair color. Some of the girls peeked out the window as if hoping for a glimpse of the prince, but most stayed still.

"It feels awkward to talk about it," said Miri, breaking the silence. "I don't like feeling in competition with everybody to be seen and liked by Prince Steffan."

"We should make a pact," said Esa. "We'll be happy for whomever he chooses, no jealousy or meanness."

All the girls agreed, but Britta seemed not to have heard and stared at the wall, her back to Esa.

"Britta?" said Miri.

"What's wrong?" asked Frid.

"She won't agree to our bargain," said Katar. "She's already bitter, it seems."

Britta rubbed her temple with the back of her hand. "It's not that. I'm just not feeling well."

Miri touched her forehead. "You are kind of warm. Maybe you should lie down."

That night, whenever Miri awoke from anxious dreams, she heard girls shifting on their pallets, readjusting pillows, sighing. Twice she saw Britta's eyes open as well.

"Are you all right?" she whispered.

"I feel funny," Britta whispered back. "Maybe I'm just nervous."

By morning, Britta's cheeks felt awfully hot to the brush of Miri's fingertips. They were confined to their bedchamber while the noise of preparation went on just outside their door, but Miri sneaked out to find Knut.

All over the building, women and men in brown-and-green clothing were sweeping, dusting, laying rugs and hanging tapestries, stoking fires in the hearths, and making the building warmer and livelier than Miri had known was possible. She kept her eyes down, hoping that if she did not make eye contact, no one would notice her enough to order her back to the bedchamber.

On her way to the kitchen, she passed the dining hall. The tables were covered in cloth and set at the far end of the room, leaving most of the smooth linder floor open for dancing. Three men hoisted a chandelier with dozens of candles to the ceiling, and candle stands as tall as quarrymen stood along the walls, waiting to be lit.

The door on the opposite side of the hall led to a section of the academy that now served as chambers for the prince and other guests. Miri could see a group standing there, and she slowed her walk to spy them out.

Several men, some as young as she, some with

white beards, conversed together. In their midst was a boy with dark hair, a long nose, and a square chin. He stood straight as though aware of his importance, and even the old men nodded to him in a respectful manner. Just before she passed by, he turned, and their eyes met. Her heart jumped, and she scurried faster.

She found Knut tugging on his beard and gripping his stirring spoon as a horde of strangers took over his kitchen. She caught his sleeve and led him out, explaining on the way what was wrong with Britta.

"She's sick all right," said Knut when he knelt beside her. "Came on fast, did it? Nerves will do that. Nothing to worry about, I don't think. She might improve by tonight."

He instructed the girls to put a cool, damp cloth on her head, change it every so often, and give her sips of cold water. So the girls passed the morning tending to Britta, fussing with their hair, cleaning their nails, and taking turns with the bathwater. When the yellow blaze of afternoon poured through their window, two seamstresses from the prince's party entered with arms full of gowns. The room hushed at once.

The older of the two seamstresses looked around and crunched her white curls inside her fist. "So many! Well, let's see what we can do to make each one of you look like a princess."

Miri tried to help Britta up, but as soon as she was sitting, Britta leaned over and vomited water.

"Better leave her be," said the younger seamstress. "She won't be able to dance a step."

"But she can't miss the ball," said Miri.

The seamstress shrugged. "And she can't attend it like that, can she? Still, sounds like the prince will be staying a few days. She's bound to be better tomorrow and can take her turn wooing him."

The seamstresses sorted through the dresses and called up different girls to be fitted. The largest dress went to Frid, and even that was not big enough to fit across her shoulders comfortably. Frid did not seem to notice. She fingered the frills on her sleeves and bodice, shook her skirts, and let her mouth hang open in awe. When she looked into the seamstress's mirror, her face beamed.

"I never felt pretty before," she said so quietly that only the seamstress and Miri could hear.

The younger seamstress was fitting Esa into a dark purple gown that made her eyes look violet and as big as a doe's.

"I said, lift up your left arm," Miri heard the seamstress say.

"I can't," said Esa.

"Why . . . ?" The seamstress's expression softened.

"Oh, have a blessed arm, do you? I've a bit of silk that will fit that dress like sunshine on water."

Miri had never seen silk before, but she had read that it was the linder of cloth, and when the seamstress pulled a silk scarf from her bag, Miri could see why. It was heavy with brilliant colors swirled into a pattern of flowers yet shimmered secretly, like water under a crescent moon. The seamstress wrapped the scarf around Esa's torso expertly, tying her left arm to her body so that it no longer hung limp.

The older seamstress smiled. "Well, aren't you a pleasant sight?"

Esa's smile seemed big enough to break loose.

All the girls were dressed, swirling their skirts and spinning and laughing, as colorful and beautiful as the painting of the house, yet Miri still sat on the floor in her well-worn woolens. The older lady sighed and sat down as though her bones would shift out of place if she moved too fast. The younger seamstress gathered up spare slippers and trimmed threads. After she was done she turned, her hands on her hips, and faced Miri.

"Now, you," she said.

Miri felt a shy smile take her lips. "I thought I was forgotten."

"How could we forget you? You're the special one."

Miri tingled to her toes.

The seamstress stepped out of the room and returned with the silver gown. In its folds it was so dark that the light parts seemed to shimmer. The seamstress held one of the pink ribbons up to Miri's face and said, "This shade fairly shouts out the rose hues in your skin. If I was asked to make a dress for you, I'd have made it this exact color."

She put it on Miri inside out, marked the seams, and sewed them tighter. Miri felt her face burn when the seamstress had to raise the hem two hands.

She slid the finished article over Miri's head and arranged it around her hips and against her ankles. The fabric felt like bathwater against her skin. She wanted to coo at herself in amazement and delight, having never imagined just how different she would feel by wearing such a dress. The cloth was the hue of the silver texture in new linder and the rosebud ribbons pink like miri flowers—in that gown she felt like the best of Mount Eskel.

The seamstress took extra time with Miri, fixing her brown hair up on her head, pinning cloth rosebuds over her ears and brow. At last she held up the mirror, but Miri kept her eyes down. She wanted to imagine that she looked as pretty as she felt.

The seamstress laughed, as if guessing Miri's thoughts.

"You are lovely, miss. You all are. If you want my wisdom, though no one ever does, forget the prince and enjoy yourselves."

Miri tried her best to ignore the nervous grumble in her stomach and how her cold hands felt as if they trembled even though they looked still. But when the light from their bedchamber window deepened, the sky was rich as wet soil and bluer than anyone's eyes, and the hour they had prepared for that past year finally arrived, Miri found she could not pretend anything past absolute panic.

Olana entered in a dark brown dress of fine cloth with skirts so long, they swept the floor. She looked so natural and even lovely in her finery, Miri guessed some of what the tutor must have given up in coming to Mount Eskel.

"It's time, girls," said Olana. "Line up, Miri is first."

Katar pushed her way to the front, just behind Miri. Miri felt as obvious as a mouse on a rock during the hawks' dinner hour, and she took steadying breaths and thought of Pa and Marda and the house with a garden.

"Will you check on Britta later?" Miri asked Olana. "She's asleep now, but she might feel better when she wakes and she could join—"

Music swept in from the hall.

"Yes, now go," said Olana, giving Miri a push.

Miri lurched forward, nearly stepped on her skirt, righted herself, and with a pounding heart strode down the corridor, toe to heel, toe to heel.

Chapter Eighteen

Call your heart to pulse
To the drum's eager beat
Hear the mountain call
Lift your arms, slide your feet

The first thing Miri noticed was the music, a sound so luscious that just hearing it reminded her of eating fresh strawberries. In front of the hearth, four women played stringed instruments that sang out in tones so round and lively, Miri could scarcely believe they were in any way related to the village's twangy, three-stringed yipper. The sounds vibrating from each musician's fingers intertwined, making something unified and beautiful that reached to Miri and called her closer in. The music held her.

She blinked and took in a room as bright as morning. Hundreds of candles flamed in the chandelier and candle stands, a fire blazed in the long hearth, the light from all sides burning away any shadows. Tapestries in vivid colors covered the walls, making the hall feel warm and alive. Their vibrancy was surpassed by the shades of the attending women's long gowns and the men's shirts, breeches, and feathered hats. A draft carried a rush of smells—meat cooking in the kitchens, perfumed soap, the delicious scent of beeswax candles. Stepping into all that color and light and music and fragrance felt like walking into an embrace.

Except that every person in that room was looking right at her. Including the prince. Miri swallowed.

The chief delegate stood by the door.

"Presenting Miri Larendaughter of Mount Eskel, the academy princess," he said.

The prince stood across the room and bowed at Miri's curtsy. She turned to the girls behind her and smiled with wide, panicked eyes before taking her place at the end of the hall. At the doorway, Katar stepped forward, smiling with dimples Miri had never before seen.

"Presenting Katar Jinsdaughter of Mount Eskel."

And so each girl stepped forward, heard her name, curtsied, and took her place along the wall. The prince bowed the same shallow bow each time, his expression stiff, even, Miri noticed, when he first caught sight of beautiful Liana.

The chief delegate introduced the last girl, and the

music changed to something light and rhythmic. The prince hesitated as he looked over the girls, but he crossed the room to Miri.

"Will you accompany me in this dance?" he said, bowing and holding out his hand.

"No, thank you." Miri smiled.

The prince frowned and looked back at the chief delegate as if for assistance.

Miri laughed self-consciously. "I, uh, I was teasing," she said, wishing now that she had not tried to make a joke. "Of course I would be honored to dance, Your Highness."

The frown relaxed from his brow, and he seemed almost to smile. He took her hand and led her to the dance floor. She hoped her palms were not terribly clammy.

The younger men from the prince's party engaged half of the academy girls for the dance. The music wrapped back to its cheery opening, the prince bowed, Miri curtsied, and they began to perform "Butterfly and Morning Glory," which she had practiced to Olana's raspy humming all summer.

Miri was so determined to get the steps right, she barely noticed her partner. When the music swelled, indicating the end of the first part, she realized that half their dance was over and he had not spoken a word. She supposed it was left to her.

"The music is beautiful. Do you like dancing, Your Highness?"

"Yes, I do," he said, his tone amiable if slightly distracted. "Do you have many chances to dance in your village?"

Miri tried not to grimace. When practicing Conversation, it was so bothersome trying to deflect direct questions about herself. She brightened as she thought of the response: "None as elegant as tonight's."

The dance required Miri to release her partner and walk behind a line of girls. They gave her questioning looks, and she shrugged as if to say she did not know what to make of him.

"There you are," she said as she emerged. "What a journey! I got lost taking a tour of the seaside." He smiled quickly, like a lightning flash in a night sky that left only an impression.

"How was your own journey up the mountain, Prince Steffan?"

He held her left hand and turned her around twice. Her skirt brushed his legs. She imagined dancing this way with Peder—not separated by a ribbon, hands touching.

"It was long, but I love seeing the country. How do

you survive such cold weather up here?"

She put her left hand on his chest. He put his left hand on her lower back.

"It's not so cold now as it will be in a month. I've never been to the lowlands. Do you like the mountains, forest, or seaside best?"

He pressed her back, turning her body to face outward as they walked.

"The seaside is very nice in summer. Have you ever been to the sea?"

They exchanged partners with the couple to their left, turned, and returned. The prince held both her hands.

"No, I haven't."

"I did not think so."

The music flourished and fell silent. It was over, and she had said nothing important at all and did not know him any better than she had before.

His apparent disinterest had not helped, she thought sourly. Perhaps he had danced "Butterfly and Morning Glory" hundreds of times and did not ponder that for her it was something special. She wanted to say, "Shame on you," as Marda had said to Bena's younger brother after he had killed a pretty little bird with his sling. But she did not. He was a prince, after all.

"It was a pleasure," he said, offering another short, stiff bow.

"The pleasure was mine, Your Highness," she said properly. Though it was not.

The prince left Miri in the center of the dance floor feeling as if she had just tumbled down a hillside. Despite practicing all summer, the girls had never thought to ask what to do when the dance was over. Miri recognized the overture for "Evening Shadows" and scurried out of the way as the prince escorted Katar to the center of the floor. At least he seemed as remote with Katar as he had with her.

Miri thought of going to check on Britta, but one of the prince's escorts, a man with short reddish hair and a face full of freckles, asked her to dance. After that she never found herself idle.

Miri observed Esa's turn with the prince, wincing in apprehension, but he was as stoically polite with Esa as he had been with Katar and Miri. He never glanced at Esa's lame arm, held her left elbow instead of her hand, and led her gracefully through the dance. Esa's smile was genuine, and in that Miri found much in Prince Steffan to admire.

Miri's other dance partners were more appealing than the prince. Many spoke freely about the provinces of Danland, the capital, and their profession as a personal guard, delegate, or courtier. A couple let slip some dismissive words regarding Mount Eskel, but most seemed awed by the view and curious about life there. Despite the disappointing prince, Miri could not feel glum.

So Miri twirled and spun, paraded and curtsied, talked and smiled, and even laughed. Her dress made the most scrumptious swish whenever she whirled around. The candles were scented with the perfume of some foreign flower, and the smell poured over everything. The music was so beautiful that it entered her with a pleasant tang, like drinking ice-melt water on an empty stomach.

Even while sitting beside the unresponsive Prince Steffan at the banquet, Miri could not relax her smile. They ate fresh roast with bread-and-vinegar pudding, pickled beetroot, lamb's head and boar's head, fresh fish breaded in wheat flour and fried with yellow squash, and heaps of soft, steamy bread. While feasting, Miri thought that she might be quite happy married to any lowlander in the kingdom if she could enjoy dinners such as this.

After the meal, servants set sweet foods on trays all over the room, and it seemed there were enough sugary things to fill the world. The musicians played melodies that yearned and pleaded, as sweet as the sticky honey cakes, syrupy custards, and fruit dusted with sugar so light that it melted on Miri's tongue before she was scarcely aware of the flavor. She looked up from biting into a fried fig to see a minister whispering urgently into the prince's ear and gesturing her way. She swallowed and brushed any crumbs from her face.

The prince approached her and bowed short and shallow. Again. Miri wondered if he tired of bowing so often and in exactly the same way.

"Miss Miri, would you care to take a turn with me?"

Miri and Steffan strolled the quiet corridors, conversing much as they had while dancing. The principles of Conversation did not work as well with the prince as they had with Peder at spring holiday. He continued to ask about her village, and after a time she ceased averting his inquiries.

She led him into the pleasant chill of the autumn night to walk the stony paths around the building. Thin fog enclosed the academy, so Miri described the view, a string of mountains so familiar that she thought of them as aunts and uncles, extensions of her own family. She told him about Marda and Pa, the people most precious to her, and about the quarry and the hard life on the mountain, but how it was even now improving.

"We may earn more next season than we used to in

three. It never occurred to us that it was possible until I happened on some information about Commerce in the academy's books. Now we have a real chance of making things better, and some villagers might be free to pursue things besides quarrying, like sculpting stone . . . or all kinds of things."

"That sounds very nice," said Steffan. "Your village must be proud of you."

"Yes, I suppose. Your Highness." She looked him over, hurt by the indifference in his tone. But why should he care? As Olana had let them know, compared with the rest of the kingdom, Mount Eskel was a bug bite on the king's ankle. Steffan could not gauge what a difference the change in trading would make and did not know how much it had meant to Miri to be a part of it.

He did not know her, and, she recognized now, he did not want to.

She stopped walking. "Why are you here?"

Steffan straightened his jacket. "Why do you address me like this?"

"Because I want to know the answer." She put her hands on her hips. "Really, why did you come?"

"I'm not accustomed to being spoken to in such a tone."

"Well, you're on Mount Eskel now, Your Highness.

I'm sorry if I'm offending you, but I've been preparing for today for a year, and I think you owe me at least some explanation of your behavior."

"I am here, as you know, because the priests have proclaimed this village the home of my bride-to-be . . ."

"Yes, yes. But do you really want to meet her? If so, then why aren't you looking at me, or at anyone, and really listening?"

Steffan frowned. "I apologize if I seem uninterested."

"Well, you do. But you don't need to apologize." Miri sat on the academy steps. "I honestly want to understand why, if you're here to discover your bride, you don't seem to be trying."

Steffan shrugged, then sighed, and his hard, princely demeanor slid off. For the first time, Miri saw an eighteen-year-old boy who could be confused like any other person. He sat beside her, stared at his boots, and rubbed a scuff mark off the leather.

"I guess this isn't what I was expecting," he said.

"What were you expecting?"

"Something more straightforward." There was a hint of alarm in his eyes. "There are so many girls in there. How am I supposed to know all of you? I hoped that one girl would just seem right. There wouldn't be explanations and awkward conversations. We would both just know."

Miri blinked. "Is this an awkward conversation?"

Steffan let himself smile. "No, this is all right."

"It's all right because you're acting like a person instead of a stone column."

"You're right to scold me, but this is a very delicate situation to be in."

Miri was tempted to roll her eyes, but she thought of the principles of Conversation and tried to see the situation from his point of view. "I can imagine that it might be overwhelming. There's only one of you, but you have to get to know twenty of us."

"Yes, exactly!" Steffan smiled at her, and she found his dull appearance much improved.

"Certainly when I imagine the reverse situation, I shudder—only one of me and twenty Prince Steffans . . . ugh."

He stared at her, not a speck of humor in his eyes.

"I'm teasing you!" She nudged him with her elbow. "I was trying to make you smile again, it was such a treat."

"Oh, I thought you were serious," he said. "Because you know I am one of twenty brothers, and we're all named Steffan."

Now it was Miri's turn to stare.

He pointed at her and raised his eyebrows. "Ah-ha!

Now the predator is prey."

"I didn't really believe that you had nineteen brothers. . . . Well, I considered it for a moment."

She nudged him again and he nudged her back, which made her laugh, and then he laughed.

"Has anyone ever told you that you have a laugh that makes others want to laugh?"

"Doter, my neighbor, always says, 'Miri's laugh is a tune you love to whistle.'"

"Well said. I would pay a deal of gold to have your talent of making other people smile." His natural confidence added weight to everything he said. Miri swallowed. A compliment from a prince felt as heavy as a mountain. "You know, you don't need to be the academy princess to make an impression."

"I make an impression because I'm so short," she said, hiding how flattered she felt.

"No, it's because you seem so happy and comfortable. It's easy to say that I enjoyed dancing and talking with you tonight more than with anyone else."

She opened her mouth to say something disparaging about herself, but her heart was thumping, and she was afraid her voice would shake, and then she remembered one of the rules of Conversation—*Be gracious to compliments.*

"Thank you," she said.

"I mean it," he said. "I really do."

They sat in silence, and Miri had time to wonder why his voice had sounded sad, almost regretful. But the night was cool and dark, and he was warm sitting next to her, and she let what he had said repeat in her mind again and again. He had enjoyed being with her the most. She was the favorite. And she, Miri of Mount Eskel, was sitting next to the prince heir of Danland as casual as anything. What an amazing night.

Chapter Nineteen

She put a wedge beside my heart
And then she brought the mallet down
She sang no song to guide her work
I lost my heart without a sound

The next morning, Miri scarcely spoke. She sat by the window and listened to the swells and whispers of conversation that filled their bedchamber like wind fills a chimney. Other girls had held private talks with the prince after Miri, and they exchanged details, how polite he was, how handsome. Others complained that he was distant and plain.

"He was kind," said Esa, "but I don't know yet if I'd want to marry him. I hope we get more chances to talk over the next few days."

"I don't need to know him any more," said Bena, yawning without bothering to cover her mouth. The prince had led her through one dance and not spoken to her again. "I thought princes were supposed to be more interesting than other boys, but he was as boring as watered-down porridge."

"*I* thought he was nice," said Liana. Bena glared at her, and Miri wondered if the friendship would survive their first disagreement.

Knut served them breakfast in their bedchamber. Britta was feeling much better, and she sat up and ate.

"Tell me what you thought of the prince," she said to Miri.

"Nice," said Miri. "At first I was awed by him; then I thought he was dull and a little rude. But he was just nervous. I like him pretty well."

Britta leaned in and whispered so the other girls could not hear, "Did he ask you . . . ?"

Miri shook her head and whispered back, "But he said he liked me best of all the girls he danced with." She shut her eyes tight to hide from the thought before she could blush.

"Of course he did!" said Britta.

"If he liked me best," Miri whispered, "do you think that means . . . ?"

Olana entered then, letting the bedchamber door slam behind her, and Miri wondered what they could have done to upset her already that morning.

"The chief delegate would like to address you," said Olana. "Stand properly, never mind your beds. If you haven't smoothed your blankets, it's too late now.

Head up, Gerti. Not so high, Katar. You look like a soldier."

She opened the door to admit the chief delegate. He glanced around the room without seeming to see the girls, though Miri thought his gaze paused for a moment on her face. She curled her toes in her boots.

"Prince Steffan bade me greet you this morning and convey the pleasure he took in your company last night. He had high praise for this academy and compliments for the quality of young ladies on Mount Eskel."

Some of the girls giggled. Miri felt frozen by the anticipation of what he would say next.

"However," said the chief delegate, and with that one word Miri felt all her self-confidence drain from her like the cold feeling she sometimes got by standing up too fast.

"However, the prince regrets that he must return to Asland today. He will revisit soon to make his choice."

In the shocked silence, Miri could hear a horse neigh a long way off.

"But it could snow very soon, maybe next week or the next," said Katar, barely above a whisper. "Then you couldn't get back up the pass until spring."

"Then the prince will return in spring," said the chief delegate.

He adjusted his collar, which appeared to be pinching his neck uncomfortably, bowed, and took his leave. Only a handful of girls recollected themselves enough to curtsy in return. Miri was not one of them.

As soon as the door shut, conversation moaned all over the room. The sound of it reminded Miri of one of the songs the musicians had played the night before. It had been a sad song, and the instruments had creaked and wailed disappointment.

"Are you all right?" asked Britta.

Miri nodded, but her head felt light and giddy. For a slim moment, she had actually believed that she would leave the mountain, become someone new, see and do great things. Now her barely realized dreams of becoming the princess emptied liked tipped jars, and she felt as though she sat in the puddle.

"I thought he was going to stay longer," said Britta. "I was sure he'd make his choice before leaving."

Miri nodded again, too humiliated to speak or even meet Britta's eyes. She leaned against their bedchamber window and watched the men and women who had accompanied the prince tear down the tents, saddle and harness the horses, pack up their goods, and start down the winding road away from the academy.

The prince's carriage was near the back, its curtains

down. She kept her eyes on a swaying gold tassel that knocked against the curtain. This time, she did not wave.

A shout from Olana brought silence to the room.

"Apparently, you failed to polish yourselves sufficiently this past year."

"Did he say that?" asked Frid. "Is that why he went home without choosing?"

"What else could this mean?" asked Olana. Her face was blotchy red, and Miri guessed she was mortified that her students had failed to measure up and frustrated that she could not return home. "The chief delegate left supplies and fuel for the winter and instructed me to continue this academy until the prince's return. You must study harder and improve yourselves by next spring."

A collective groan went up. Miri felt as withered as a winter carrot just thinking of being locked up in the academy again through the cold months. Last night he had been so kind. What had changed?

She thought of running home or chasing after the prince and demanding an answer, but she just slipped outside alone.

Some minutes later, Miri was scratching letters on a large stone when someone came jogging from the direction of the village. He slowed when he neared, and Miri found herself stunned for the second time that day when she saw that it was Peder. She was used to having the idea of Peder nestled constantly inside all she did, but she realized now that since her talk with Steffan all thoughts of Peder had flitted away.

He looked around as if expecting to see more activity. "I thought the prince would've come by now."

"He did." Miri threw a rock shard as far as she could. It hit another stone and cracked into more pieces. "Came and went."

"Oh." Peder looked at his feet, then at Miri, then at his feet again. "Did he choose you?"

"He didn't choose anyone," Miri said more harshly than she meant to.

"Sounds like you're upset about that."

"Well, he shouldn't make us all live in this drafty building practicing curtsies and stupid Poise and make us all believe we could be a princess, then just come and leave again, as though we're not worthy of him. As though he's disappointed."

"So, that's it?" said Peder, his voice getting louder. "You wanted him to choose you."

Miri glared at Peder. "What are you yelling at me for? Now we have to stay here another winter and try to be better, but I'll fail again. I can't work in the quarry, I can't be a princess, what am I good enough for?"

"Well, if that's what you want, I hope you get it," said Peder. "I hope he comes back and carries you off to be a princess and keeps you as far away from Mount Eskel as you want to be."

Peder started to walk back toward the village, then after a few paces he tripped into a jog and then a run. Miri watched him go, at first ready to shout something nasty at his back, then losing her anger so quickly that she felt chilled by its loss. Why had he come, anyway? *To see me?* Miri wondered.

Wait, she wanted to shout, but hesitated. The distance swallowed all sign of him, and she turned and kicked a stone so hard, she cried out at the pain in her toe.

Just then, as if in response to her own cry, she heard someone wail.

Her first thought was that Olana had broken the terms and delivered another palm lashing; but no, the sound was wrong. It had been strange and sad, like an animal dying. Though she was none too eager to join whatever unhappiness was boiling inside the academy, she was curious and so crept toward the bedchamber window.

Miri had crossed half the distance when another wail unwound and then stopped short with a crash, as if someone had thrown a ceramic plate against the wall. She stopped, her skin tingling with prickles, though she could not imagine what she had to fear.

A jolt of quarry-speech thrust every other thought out of her head. It was the strongest quarry-speech she had ever heard, and it carried with it the feeling of Esa. The memory was a time when she, Esa, and other children had played Wolf and Rabbit in the village center. Miri had been the rabbit and run as fast as she could flee around the circle. She could not see the face of the wolf.

With sickening terror, Miri thought she understood. Esa was telling her to run.

Chapter Twenty

Well, the bandit man
He told his first man
Climb up and when you arrive
Leave no mountain man
Alive, no, leave no man alive

Miri did not wait to learn more. If Esa said to run, then she would run. Peder would be just minutes ahead, and perhaps she could catch him. The rocky path she had run on her entire life suddenly felt as treacherous as sprinting through mud, and she wished with all her breath that she could fly as the hawk, though she did not know what she was running from.

She passed the bend in the road and hoped to see Peder just ahead, but the road stretched long before her with no one in sight. After leaving her, he must have kept running.

Then she heard the someone behind her. At first she hoped that she was hearing her own echoes, but no, the rhythm of bootfalls was different, faster. She peered back and saw a man she did not know. He was getting closer.

She would have screamed for Peder if she could, but fear constricted her throat and the effort to flee used up all her breath. She tried to focus on making her feet spring over the rocks and her legs pump her forward, though fright began to gnaw at her hope. She knew she was caught even before the rough hands reached out to seize her.

She kicked and screamed and tried to get her teeth into his hand, but she was so small and her attacker so strong. He carried her back to the academy writhing under his arm and dumped her on the floor of the bedchamber.

"I found this one outside," said her attacker, his breath wheezing in his throat. "Gave me quite a run, the little rodent."

The girls sat on the floor. Knut was leaning against a wall and holding his arm as though it might be broken above the wrist. The room was crowded by fifteen men in sheepskin and goatskin, leather boots tied with long cords up their thighs, and fur-lined caps. Some had golden loops in their ears, some carried cudgels and staves. They all had untidy beards and faces dirtier than an unswept floor.

"Bandits," Miri said aloud to make herself believe it. After so many years, bandits had returned to Mount Eskel.

Olana crouched in a corner, and her hands shook as they fluttered about her neck. That one detail made Miri's heart beat as if it would come loose. If Olana was scared, then the situation was very bad indeed.

The bandit nearest to Olana caught her throat in his hand and shoved her against the wall.

"You said they were all here before." His voice was low and raw, as though he had battled a chest cough for months on end. "Count them again, this time as though your life depended on it, because, in fact, it does. Is anyone else missing?"

Olana scanned the room, her eyes scarcely blinking. She shook her head. The man smiled with dirty teeth.

"I believe you this time," he said. "How fortunate for you."

He let her go and turned to face the rest of them. He was larger than most of the other bandits, though Miri noted that none looked as large as her father, Os, or most Mount Eskel men. No wonder the bandits avoided attacking the village directly.

"Hello, children," he said. "If you need to address

me, you may call me Dan."

"His ma named him after the first king himself," said another, who had a thick, jagged scar from one side of his mouth up to his ear. "Hoped he'd grow up into a proper nobleman." Several of the men laughed.

"Dan suits me fine," he said amiably. "Better than Dogface."

The men laughed louder, and the scarred one called Dogface spat on the floor.

"Looks like we've some talking to do." Dan sat on his heels, rested his forearms on his thighs, and looked at the girls with a smile that made Miri's stomach feel sour. His rough voice became singsong, as though he were telling a bedtime story to small children.

"We jumped a traveling man of business a few weeks ago and gently pressed him for anything more valuable than his life. The information he had about the prince's visit to Mount Eskel was almost worth letting him go." Dan smiled at Dogface and shook his head as though sharing some private joke. "We've been watching this building for a few days now, but the prince had so many soldiers guarding his precious hide, we didn't have a chance to pounce him. No matter. When no young lady accompanied him home, I told my lieutenant here, 'How fortunate. What a gentleman that prince is to leave behind a nicety for our plucking!' And so I come to the matter at hand. Tell me, which one of you birdies is the future bride?"

His gaze dragged the room and reminded Miri of the time she had seen a wolf eyeing her rabbits.

"Speak up!" His expression raged, then just as quickly he resumed his mock-friendly demeanor. "We may look rough, but we're not ignorant. We know the prince was here to choose a bride, and once he's chosen and the betrothal sealed, it cannot be undone. A princess-to-be will provide a hefty ransom."

"The prince left without choosing," said Katar, speaking first. "He said he'd be back."

Dan stalked across the room to Katar. "That's a nice little story." He clutched her curly hair in his fist and pulled her to her feet. "Now tell me who she is."

"Ah, ah, I don't know, I mean, no one," said Katar, tears rising in her eyes. "He didn't choose anyone."

Dan let her fall to the ground. It occurred to Miri that it was the responsibility of adults to make sure everyone else was all right. But Olana just stood there looking at the ground, her lips tight with fear, and Knut bent over his arm, his eyes closed.

"There's no sense protecting the princess," said Dan. "I'll get it out of you eventually." His voice sweetened as though he spoke to a baby. "All I want is one little bitty girl, and the rest of you can go home to your families. That's not too much to ask, is it?"

It seemed futile to assert again that the prince had not chosen, so no one answered.

Without warning, Dan grabbed Gerti and pulled her upright. The one they called Dogface wrapped her wrists with rope, threw the rope over a ceiling beam, and pulled so that Gerti hung by her wrists. She cried out, a noise like a wounded goat kid.

Miri stood. "Why are you hurting her? She didn't do anything."

Miri did not see Dan hit her, she just felt herself fly. When her tilting vision straightened, she found herself on the floor, her head against the wall. Pain battered both sides of her head. She was aware that Britta was holding her hand, but the touch gave little comfort. The pain tightened, and she wanted to vomit, but she sat very still, stared at a linder floor-stone, and breathed.

"I'm not playing here," Dan was saying. "And you see that I'm not a man of patience. I want to know who will be the princess, and I want to know it before I count to twenty, or each of you will have your turn feeling the back of my hand."

Dogface tugged again on the rope, pulling Gerti higher. She whimpered. Miri lifted her head to look at Gerti but quickly looked down again when Dan turned her way. She wanted to make this stop, but her head throbbed, and the pain seemed to radiate everywhere. Her teeth began to chatter and her legs felt loose, like half-empty straw mattresses. She had never experienced any sensation like this. Real fear. She was helpless under its weight.

Miri was vaguely aware of Dan's voice counting, "Twelve, thirteen," a hard voice, and the sound of those numbers pulsed in her headache. She knew that something bad would happen when he stopped counting, but she did not believe she could do anything to prevent it.

Then Frid stood up slowly, crossing her arms, her feet wide apart as if daring anyone to knock her down. Miri expected Frid to challenge Dan to fight or threaten him or even curse him, but instead she looked him straight in the eye and said what Miri least expected.

"It's me."

Dan stopped counting. "He picked you?"

Frid nodded. "He took me aside after we danced. He asked me not to tell anyone, so I didn't speak up earlier, but it's true. I'm going to be the princess."

Frid's lower lip twitched and her stare was too bold. Miri guessed that this was the first time Frid had ever lied.

"Now then, that wasn't so hard." He squinted at

Frid and made a face as though he sucked on something sour. "There's no accounting for taste, though, is there?"

Some of the men laughed. Frid blinked a little longer than normal, the only indication Miri could see that his comment hurt her.

Miri did not know what would have happened if Frid had not spoken up; perhaps Dan would have beaten them all, perhaps he would have killed Gerti as an example. He believed that the prince had chosen a bride and would not cease his hunt until he had discovered her.

Clearly, Frid supposed Dan would take her away and let the other girls go free, that it was better to sacrifice herself than risk everyone. It might be so, but Miri found herself remembering an account she had read in one of Olana's books. Decades before, bandits had set upon a king's traveling party in a wood. They had taken the king for ransom and left his men and horses tied to trees. Before other travelers came upon them, over half of the party died of thirst.

Miri wondered if Dan truly would let the other girls go and risk their families hunting down the bandits or if would he leave them tied up in the academy to die from the cold or thirst, or even hurry death's job.

Perhaps he would release them; perhaps a village three hours away posed no threat. Even if he did, Miri quaked to imagine what kinds of things would happen to Frid if she went alone. But what if they could keep Dan guessing, if he could not be certain who was the princess?

Keeping her eyes on Frid for courage, Miri pulled herself to her feet. The ache in her head made her wobble, and she leaned on the wall for support.

"You must be lying," said Miri. "The prince told me at the ball that he would marry me. He said he'd announce it in the spring."

Frid clenched her jaw. "No, he told me I'd be the princess."

Miri could see that Frid was willing to be the martyr, but Miri would not let her. "That's impossible, because he told me the same thing."

Dan growled. "I'm heating up to whip the liar, so which one of you is it?"

Frid and Miri pointed at each other. "She is," they said at once.

Miri tried to catch eyes with the other girls and prod them to act with a look. Britta was staring at Miri, her mouth slightly agape, then understanding resolved her features. She stood.

"I don't believe either of you," she said in a tiny

voice. "He chose me."

"How dare you?" said Katar. She was fighting a smile, as though she actually enjoyed it all. "I don't think a prince would lie, and he told me he chose me."

That unleashed every voice in the room, and girls leapt to their feet, each shouting that she was the princess. Some of the girls pushed each other, feigning anger. Even Gerti kicked her feet and shouted, "Let me down! The prince will be furious if he hears how you treated his future bride!"

Dogface let go of Gerti's rope, and she slumped to the floor. Dan looked around the room, his face bewildered.

"Enough!" he shouted. The girls quieted except for one belated "Me, me!" from Esa, who blushed.

Dan rubbed his beard. "Either they're lying or that prince took pleasure from sweet-talking all the girls just to disappoint them later. Except one. But which one? Any guesses?"

His men pointed to one or another of the girls in halfhearted speculation.

"Since we don't know, we'll have to take them all, won't we? We'll rest here tonight and head out in the morning." Dan huddled in the corner of the room and conversed with his lieutenant, a short, hairy man named Onor. Miri could not hear the words, but the sound of their talk pricked her with dread. She wished she could find a reason to laugh.

"A palm lashing and a closet suddenly don't seem so bad," she whispered. Esa chuckled without any merriment. A bandit hushed them.

In silence, the girls watched the afternoon fade. The hearth fire burned a shallow warmth, its uneven light filling the room with moving shadows. Britta rested her head on Miri's lap. Frid and Esa wrapped Knut's broken arm tight to his body to keep it still. He fell asleep, his face tense and lined, as though it were only with great effort that he could sleep through the pain.

Miri's own head had never ceased pounding, and she did not think she could rest. But when she lay down and closed her eyes, she found she wanted nothing more than to forget where she was, and her body let her.

Chapter Twenty-one

Then the mountain shrugged
And the mountain yawned
Its voice was a hiss of steam
That sank into every
Dream, yes, sank deep in each dream

That night, winter came early. Snowfall slowed the morning's arrival, and the groggy gray light finally filtered out the night some hours past dawn. The view from the window showed a world lost to a storm of snowflakes thick as ash thrown from a bonfire. It was enough to change Dan's mind—they would stay at the academy until the storm broke.

The bandits allowed the girls to keep the hearth fire burning, but the chill crawled in through the stones, and the girls huddled in cold and fear in the center of the room. Dan had locked Olana and Knut in a separate room so that "the grown ones won't be inciting the young ones." When the bandits paid them little mind, the girls risked whispered conversations.

"I'm sorry now that we sent the soldiers away," said Esa.

Frid tilted her head, considering. "No, two soldiers wouldn't have stopped this lot and would've gotten killed trying to protect us, I think."

"Esa, your brother was here yesterday." Miri froze at a noise, but it was just the wind whooping and plunging in the chimney. She continued in an even softer voice. "I told him about the prince and staying at the academy until his return in the spring."

"That means no one from the village will be coming anytime soon," Britta whispered.

"My pa will come," said Gerti. "He wouldn't just let Olana keep me another winter."

"Not in that snow he won't," said Katar.

Esa nodded. "Your pa doesn't know we're in danger, Gerti. Even if he plans to come and get you, he'd wait until the snow stops. They all would. But by the time they get to the academy, the bandits will have us halfway to—"

Dan rushed across the pallets and lifted Esa from the ground with just one hand around her neck. He spoke so close to her face, she flinched from the spittle flying from his mouth. "You talk again, I make sure you can't talk at all."

Then he smiled his sick, mock smile and put her

down as gently as if she were a newborn baby. Miri sat on her hands and glared at the floor.

After another day of snow, the bandits discovered the academy's winter food storage. More and more of them left the bedchamber and returned with heaping plates of food—roasted pork and liver sausage; loose salads of turnips, potatoes, carrots, and apples; jerky stew with onions. The constant smell of roasting meat was agonizing to Miri's rumbling stomach. The bandits gave the girls watery wheat porridge.

Whenever the men watched the window and the snow that continued to fall, Miri noticed tension tighten their brows, but otherwise they seemed content to stay for the winter, eating all day and playing a game involving little cubes and stones. They talked in hushed tones, glaring at the girls.

Two of the men whispered to each other in voices too low for Miri to hear, but apparently Dan could.

"Speak up!" he shouted, shoving one of the bandits against the wall. "You have a concern, you tell me to my face, not whisper about it like little boys."

The bandit lowered his head deferentially. "Easy now, Dan. I was just wondering what we were doing holed up in here, like we were just waiting for their pappies to come save them."

Dan let his face set hard before he spoke. "Nobody's

going to walk miles in that snowstorm, and I'm not marching out in it, either. We'll stay here until the weather clears, then we'll march them down to our main camp."

"That's a lot of hostages to feed," said the bandit.

"But it'll be worth it once the king pays ransom for his son's betrothed. Besides, we won't hold them long."

Dan turned and caught Miri looking at him. She flinched.

"Then we'll let the little princesses go home," he said, his rough, low voice straining to sound sweet.

Miri tried to swallow, but her mouth was too dry.

Without seeming to, she kept an eye on Dan. She sat on the pallet closest to the bandits and watched him with eyes half-closed. Often he paced about and roared at his men. When he was still, he turned to the window, and the silvery light of a snow day did not reach the dark puckers of scars in his cheeks. His eyes ticked as if trying to track the falling flakes. Though he was sitting, his whole body was tight, a rope pulled as taut as iron. Miri felt her own body tense just watching him, afraid of what he might do when he sprang.

The evening of the third day, Miri observed Dan scratch at his beard and rub his neck, stand up, and pace. She inched back on her pallet. He cursed and swung at a chair that stood in his way, sending it cracking against a wall. That did not seem to relieve his agitation enough, so he cursed again and reached out to the closest girl, dark-haired Liana. Before his hands seized her neck, Onor stood between them.

"Not now." Onor spoke in tones almost too low for Miri to hear. He pushed Dan's chest, trying to calm him. "Don't kill anyone now. There will be plenty of time later."

Dan spat to the side in frustration. He glared at Liana, who scuttled out of his way and curled up against the wall.

"I've got to get out of this room," he said to Onor, though still glaring at Liana. "You watch them."

Dan slammed the door behind him, and Onor settled in the corner, his eyes on the girls. *There will be plenty of time later*. Miri filled in the rest of Onor's statement: *For killing*.

Doter often said, *Truth is when your gut and your mind agree,* and a heaviness in Miri's gut confirmed what she was starting to believe—if the bandits took them down the mountain, none of them would return. They had to run, and soon.

Miri waited until it was night and only three men were guarding the girls. Two were playing a quiet game, throwing marked pebbles off the wall. One slouched low to the floor, his eyes covered by a cap, his breathing like the creak of a door opened slowly. She could not bear the tension another moment and did not dare wait until Dan lost his temper and killed someone. They had to chance it.

Miri hummed a quarry tune, lying on her side and resting her head on her hand. She pressed her other hand against a floorstone. One of the bandits glanced her way, then looked back to his game.

To the bandit, she appeared only to hum and lounge. Inside, she sang out in quarry-speech. *Rabbits, run!* Her body was tense, her blood felt cold. She waited until every girl looked at her and seemed ready. Then she grabbed Britta's hand and took to her feet. By the time she crossed the threshold, she saw that only half the girls had followed her down the corridor. It was too late to stop now. She looked forward and concentrated on escape.

The linder floorstones felt slick beneath her in the darkness, as though she skated on ice. Her breath came hard, and she focused on chasing the misty huff she pushed before her with each exhale. She could hear the startled cries of two or three girls behind her as they were caught by the bandits at the door.

"They're running!" one shouted.

Faster, she wanted to say, but she was too terrified

to speak. Out the front door, down the steps, and suddenly outside. The cold, breezy air felt unfamiliar to her, and the uneven ground of snow over rock shards seemed as dangerous as walking on knives.

She had made it only a few paces from the building when her head jerked, her body flung out in front of her, and she fell on her back in the snow. Dogface had caught her braid. He started to pull her back to the building by her hair, and she scrambled to stand and staggered beside him. In his other hand he held Esa by her limp arm.

When Dogface dumped Miri and Esa to the floor, she counted heads with a fearful hope—twenty. None of the girls had gotten away. If only all of them had run at once.

Every bandit now stood in the bedchamber, including Dan.

"Who's your little leader?" he said, his voice even more hoarse than usual. "Tell me quick, who gave the order to run?"

"She did." Bena pointed at Miri. "She told us to escape, but some of us ignored her. She's not our leader."

The ten girls who had not run grouped together—they were all the older girls except Katar, some younger girls who were often cowed by Bena's fierceness, and thirteen-year-old Helta, who seemed too frightened to move. Bena smiled, for a moment. But then Dan looked her over, and the force of his attention was enough to make her squirm. The standing girls sat, and Liana hid her face in her hands. Miri glared. Did Bena think that by betraying her Dan would give her a pat and let her go?

One of the bandits who had been gaming in the corner spoke up. "We've been watchful, Dan, and we never heard her nor nobody say a word."

"I'm sure you didn't," said Dan with a glower. The bandit shrank back. "Dogface, Onor, come over here. I want a plan to keep these girls locked up and out of my hair until this snowstorm stops."

They clumped by the door, and Dan growled at them, reprimanding and demanding better vigilance.

"I wish I'd run home," Helta whispered, then started to cry.

"Shut up," Dan yelled at her.

Miri clenched her hands and wished that she were as strong as her pa and could knock him down like the bully he was. She knew hitting him would be useless, but she yearned to strike at him in some way, have a chance to see *him* squirm.

She waited until there was a lull in his conversation with the bandits, and then she spoke.

"Pardon me, Dan," she said meekly, though her

heartbeat roared in her ears. "Sir, I think you should know something."

Dan looked at Miri, and she tried not to fidget.

"One lifetime ago bandits came to Mount Eskel," she said.

At the sound of that phrase, all the girls looked up. It was the first line in the story told every spring holiday.

"What?" said Dan. "What are you talking about?"

"They thought to sack such a small village easily enough," said Miri, forcing her wavering voice louder to steady it. "They thought they could steal, burn, and be gone before the sun saw their deeds. But they were ignorant, tiny men. They did not know Mount Eskel's secrets."

Dan clamped his hand over Miri's mouth. "I didn't ask, and I don't care much for—"

"The mountain knows the feel of an outsider's boot, and the mountain will not support its weight," said Esa, rushing ahead to the middle of the story. All eyes turned to Esa, and her right hand quaked at the attention. Miri's heart ached with pride.

"Dogface," said Dan, and stuck out his chin to point at Esa. Dogface shut Esa's mouth, but Frid crossed her arms and continued the story.

"The mountain will not support its weight," Frid

repeated. "The bandits came nearer and nearer, and the mountain groaned in the night." Two bandits seized her, and she fought to keep talking. "It groaned, and the villagers heard and awoke."

A third bandit stuffed his cap in her mouth to silence her. She clenched and unclenched her fists as though it were only with great restraint that she kept herself from pummeling him.

"These girls are creepy," said a bandit with a scar through one eye.

"They're just trying to get under your skin," said Dan. "Don't—"

"The villagers awoke," said Katar, chin up, eyes flashing, "and they were waiting. With mallets and chisels and levers they waited. That night, the quarriers stood taller than trees, taller than mountains, and they struck like lightning. When the first bandits fell, the rest ran. They ran like hares from a hawk."

"Stop it!" said Dan. "We'll gag every one of you if we have to."

Katar started the last lines of the story, and every girl who had run with Miri joined her.

"Mount Eskel feels the boots of outsiders." They paused, and then not even Bena stayed silent for the final line. "Mount Eskel won't bear their weight."

All the men in the room stared at the girls, half

with mouths gaping, all with eyes so wide that their foreheads creased. One man rubbed his arm as though trying to get warm. Britta looked at Miri, a secret smile tensing her lips.

Then the sound of Dan applauding chilled the room. "Lovely bedtime story, and like all beddie-byes, as true as snow in summer. Tell another one, and you'll all wait in ropes for the storm to clear. I think gagging the little inciter will be enough for now."

Miri felt Dan pull a handkerchief over her mouth and tie her hands behind her back. Then he grabbed the roots of her hair and pulled her ear to his mouth.

"I know your kind." His throaty whisper gave her chills, like rat claws scurrying across her skin. "You think you're a little bandit, hm? You think you're clever? There's nothing swimming around in your head that I don't already know. I'll share with you the only thing on my mind—the next time there's trouble, I slit your throat first and ask questions later. Nothing's keeping me from my fortune. Understand, little princess?"

She did not move, so he pulled her head up and down, forcing her to nod. She tried to swallow, but the thought of a slit throat made it painful. Dan smiled as if he did indeed know what she was thinking.

You don't know everything, Miri thought fiercely, because she could not speak it aloud. *I'm no princess. I'm a Mount Eskel girl, and I know things you could never guess.* It was a weak defense, but just the thought made her feel stronger.

Dan left eight bandits to guard the girls in the bedchamber and three more just outside the door. Miri lay on her side, arranged her bound hands behind her, and kept watch as the fire burned low, dimmer than a crescent moon.

The men were quiet that evening, and Miri wondered if they were thinking about the story. She had started the telling to make them uneasy and if there was cowardice in their hearts perhaps prick them to fleeing. But now the story was giving her a bigger idea.

No matter what Dan thought, there was fact in it. Once bandits *had* come, and the villagers had beaten them soundly. She supposed the story did take some liberties, because the mountain could not really speak to them. Yet the kernel of that idea was true—quarry-speech allowed the villagers to talk through the mountain, to send their song down into the linder so another could hear. If Miri could communicate exam answers on a hill, what else was possible?

Her silent challenge to Dan heartened her. She

was a Mount Eskel girl. There was something she could do.

Miri moved her upper body off her pallet and pressed her cheek on a cold floorstone. The mountain was filled with linder. There could be veins and layers and masses of linder marbled underground, deep and shallow, a trail of it from the floorstone beneath her all the way to the village. There must be.

Her breath bounced back from the stone and warmed her face. She listened to it, caught its rhythm, and tried to form a song of her thoughts.

It was a long way to the village. She imagined the road, the many turns, past decades of dead quarries, miles of cliff edge. On the hill during the exam, the girls had all been as close as two arms' reach. The hopelessness of trying scared her, and her breath caught.

Doter always said, *Thinking it's impossible makes it so.* A year ago, just using quarry-speech outside the quarry seemed impossible. Miri shoved her doubts away.

She sang her thoughts down into the linder, sang of her family, their pallets cuddled close on a freezing night. She hoped Pa or Marda might hear her memory of home and understand that Miri needed them.

Miri tried different memories until her sticky eyelids told her it was long past midnight, when everyone in the village was surely asleep. Wakeful academy girls gave her bewildered looks, a sign that her quarry-speech brushed through them; though not knowing the specific memory she used, they most likely had thoughts of their own firesides. But from far away, Miri sensed no response. Her bound hands were asleep, her neck and shoulder throbbed from lying on the floor, her middle was tight with hunger. When the discomfort overwhelmed her concentration, she twisted back onto her pallet and slept fitfully.

The gloomy light of another snowy morning woke her, and she renewed her labor. All day and into that night, she tried every way she could imagine. She quarry-spoke memories only her father knew and days she had spent with Marda alone. Stillness answered.

Britta sat beside Miri and smoothed her brow, slipping aside her gag to offer her sips of water when no bandit looked their way. Miri could not relax; the thin muscles of her forehead were bound and tense.

"Are you sick?" Britta whispered.

Miri shook her head but could explain no more. She kept reaching out, hopelessness mixed with hope.

When afternoon light melted into the room, Miri felt nearly crazed with her effort and had to try something new. Peder came to mind, and despite their recent quarrel, she found the thought of him calming.

She closed her eyes, shook loose her thoughts, and sang into the linder of spring holiday. They were sitting on the same stone, their legs almost touching, the nearest bonfire echoing on the blacks of his eyes.

Perhaps an hour into trying, her concentration dissolved and her thoughts were snatched by a memory of a summer afternoon years before. She and Peder sat on the stream bank, their feet turning blue in the icy water. All around, the goats yanked at river grass and bleated at the sun. A small butterfly with pale wings flitted past her nose, pausing as if at first believing she were a flower. Peder plucked a wing-shaped leaf, sucked it against his lips, and blew it away. It spun and flew, dipping and rising on a breeze, and seemed to be chasing after the butterfly until it touched the surface of the stream and was pulled down and away.

There was nothing special about that day. It was just one of many from her childhood, one hour out of thousands she had spent beside Peder. But the thought of it made her feel warm. Her heart pulsed through her ribs and reminded her now, trapped and cold and afraid, what it felt like to be content. And the idea of Peder came knit with the memory, as though she caught a faint scent of him on her clothes.

There was no vibration behind her eyes; the memory was dim and strange. It was not like the quarry-speech Peder had spoken to her at spring holiday, strong and garish, images shouting behind her eyes. Yet she believed her mind was not just wandering. She felt it was Peder.

She moved completely off her pallet and pressed her whole body tight to the floor, desperate to keep communicating. The cold of the stones pierced through her clothes, but she clenched her teeth and ignored it. Closing her eyes, she sang a memory of spring holiday and the telling of the bandit story. Again and again she repeated the images of that event, forming rhythm with her thoughts, pairing them together as she would rhyme two lines of a song, singing them silently into the stone. *Bandits, danger.* She prayed Peder would understand. *Now, here at the academy—bandits, tell our parents!*

She quarry-spoke until her thoughts felt rough and grating, her mind as hoarse as her throat would be after hours of yelling. Peder did not speak back again.

Hours of silence pressed on her. Her body ached from lying on the floor, and she sat up and stretched her bound arms and realized how much her head hurt. Outside, the snow still fell.

Esa and Frid looked at her questioningly, and Miri shrugged defeat. Her temples felt as though chisels sought to square her skull like a block of linder. A bandit allowed Britta to remove Miri's gag for a moment and feed her porridge; then despondency made her sleepy, and she lay down and dreamed of climbing a slope that had no peak.

Chapter Twenty-two

The boot prints were pricks
In the mountain's side
So the mount it roared a stone groan
And made those bandits
Moan, yes, made them shake and moan

Miri awoke with such a jolt that she sat upright. Had someone called her? Her breath sounded so loud to her own ears, she was afraid a bandit might come over to investigate. Slowly, aching at the crinkling of her pallet, she lay back down.

No one had spoken aloud, she was certain now, yet she still had the impression of her name pulsing in her head. She listened—the soft sounds of sleep, raspy snarls of snores, crackle of bodies restless on straw pallets, scratching and turning, the moans of troubled slumber. No voices. A tingle behind her eyes made her believe it might have been quarry-speech, and she stayed awake, listening.

Her mind grabbed the memory of the last time she

had seen Peder, just after the prince left. They had been standing within sight of the academy before the first bend in the road. In that dark, cold room, the remembrance was so bright in her mind as to warm her limbs. She could picture how the light from the falling sun had struck Peder's eyes, making them appear all blue with no black at all, and she could feel her fists clenched at her sides.

"Ah . . ." She could not stop a small sound of wonder escaping her lips. This time there was no doubt Peder was calling to her in quarry-speech. Perhaps before, the sense of him had been faint because he had been far away. It was stronger now, much clearer. He was near, she was certain. But was he alone?

Miri rolled off her pallet to touch the linder floor, and she answered back by quarry-speaking her own memory of their last parting. His response was immediate—the mountain cat hunt. Miri was seven again, standing in her doorway, watching some thirty men and women set out to hunt down a mountain cat that had stalked the village's rabbits. They held levers, pickaxes, and mallets, and their faces were grim and determined.

Peder had brought the villagers, and they were carrying weapons.

Miri sought for a way to ask, *What should I do?* But

she knew the answer. The girls had to get out of the building. If they could make it outside, she knew the villagers would be waiting to protect them. But if their families had to storm the building, there would be fighting, perhaps even killing.

The eight bandits in the bedchamber slept, three of their bodies blocking the room's only door. Miri teetered to her feet and tiptoed to the window. The night was solid with snowfall, but as she stared into the torrent of flakes, a wind rose briefly and parted the storm. There, just before the bend in the road, she saw a line of darker shapes. To a watchful bandit they might appear just lumps of rocks, but Miri knew the shape of every rock around the academy. The villagers were there, waiting.

Miri closed her eyes and sang a quarry-speech memory of the stone hawk lying on that windowsill one spring morning. She hoped Peder would understand and watch the window.

She felt her blood rush through her, warning her that she was about to do something terrifying. *I slit your throat first and ask questions later*, Dan had said. And Miri believed him. Now, as she was about to take another step toward escape, his threat was as real and immediate as the air in her lungs.

Miri began to tremble. She leaned her shoulder

against the wall and found she could not move. The villagers were so far away on the other side of the snowfall, and Dan and his knife as near as the next room. When she had started calling out in quarry-speech, she had not imagined this part, the need to get the girls out of the academy without help and the terrible risk of being caught again.

Don't hesitate, she reminded herself. *Just strike, Miri. Just swing, mountain girl.* She chanted to herself to give her limbs courage and reasons to move. She was the academy princess. She was her ma alive again. Peder had heard her call and come in the night. Her pa would be out there, his arms strong enough to crush bandits like rubble rock. Olana and Knut were locked away, and there was no one else.

Her breath shuddered out of her chest. She took the first step.

Miri trod softly away from the window and to Britta's pallet, stooping beside her to touch her with a bound hand.

Britta opened her eyes and without making a sound looked at Miri, looked at the sleeping bandits, and nodded understanding.

She untied Miri's hands and gag, and then the two girls crawled around the room, whispering into ears and making silence gestures. Some startled awake, and the crackle of their pallets sent Miri's heart tumbling. She shot a glance at the sleeping men—none aroused.

The steady pop and crumble of the low fire masked some of the noise of girls sitting up, lacing boots, whispering anxious queries. Miri crouched before the hearth so all might see her face. She touched the floor with her fingertips and reminded them in quarry-speech of the villagers fighting the mountain cat, hoping that all of them shared the memory of that night years before. Then she pointed to the window.

She saw their faces turn to that dull point of light and flicker with apprehension and fear. Miri could not risk having anyone stay behind. With her eyebrows raised as if she posed a question, Miri pointed at each girl and waited until she nodded agreement. To her relief, even Bena did not hesitate.

As silent as owls' wings, the girls stole to the window. Far above the snow clouds, the moon must have been bright and full. Its light bled through the storm, marking each flake with a silvery luster and pouring a pale, peachy glow onto the mountain. Just out of sight, she believed her pa and others stood ready.

Frid and Miri examined the wood frame of the window, looking for a place to tear it free. Bena, who was much taller than Miri, stepped forward to help Frid break the wood at the top. The crack sounded like a frantic moan, and the girls froze, watching the faces of the sleeping men. The one-eyed bandit lay not two paces away, but his good eye did not open.

Frid and Bena peeled away the rest of the wood. Much of it was damp from ice leaking through and came off without too much trouble, though Miri expected that the two girls had fingers full of splinters. Bena's hands were deft and silent, and Miri found herself thinking that Bena was a wonderful, wonderful person.

When enough of the frame was removed, they eased the glass pane free; then five girls took careful hold and lowered the window to the ground. Miri heard a collective exhale when it rested against the wall, a reaction that in other circumstances might have made her laugh. The silence instead was unnerving.

Cold air poured through the empty window. One of the bandits stirred.

Miri grabbed Liana and with Frid's and Bena's help lifted her through the window. No sooner had Liana landed outside than the line of villagers walked forward. Miri's limbs felt stronger just at the sight. Thirty or forty of them marched steadily toward the academy, and Liana ran past them and huddled safely behind. Another girl was just behind her, and another. Five girls were out now. Six.

"Why's it so cold?" called out a sleepy voice.

Panic shook Miri's hands, and she almost fell over when giving Tonna a boost. Ten girls passed through. Twelve. Sixteen.

"What the . . ." The one-eyed bandit sat up. "Dan! They're running!"

"No," Miri breathed.

Frid tossed another girl through the window, then turned to the waking bandits. One lunged for Miri, but Frid was faster. She grabbed a privy pot and broke it over his head with a noise and a stench that brought the others to their feet. Bena climbed out the window. All the girls were through now but Miri and Frid.

"Hurry!" said Miri, scrambling out on her own.

She hit the ground outside and heard Frid behind her and the shouts of the bandits that followed. Bandits were surging out the front door, and girls wailed as they were caught before they reached the villagers.

Miri ran. The villagers were so close, she felt she should be able to jump to them as easily as springing across a stream. The snow was knee-high, and her escape seemed impossibly slow, as though she lay sick somewhere far away and only dreamed of running.

The villagers were rushing forward, attempting to get to the fleeing girls before the bandits could, but Miri saw Britta yanked back and heard another girl scream to her right. There was a clatter of wood on metal that meant someone was fighting. She kept her eyes on the villagers, on her pa running to her, and pushed herself faster.

Then a hand touched her back. She cried out as she was wrenched from her flight and twisted around. Dan's scarred face sneered at her, inches from her own.

"You're the troublemaker," he said, and his mouth stank of meat. "I'll see you broken and dead."

Chapter Twenty-three

Don't look down, don't look down
In midair you drown, drown

Miri!" Her pa sprang forward. Rage distorted his face, and Miri trembled just to see it. A bandit overtook him, and Pa's mallet swung twice—once to pound the bandit's club to the ground, once to knock the bandit down. Pa hurdled him and rushed toward Dan, his mallet raised.

"I'll kill her!" said Dan, his hoarse voice straining to yell. His hands gripped Miri's neck. "I'll snap her in two, mountain man."

Pa stopped. Miri could see him tighten his hold on the mallet shaft, look to Miri, look at Dan, wanting nothing more than to beat the bandit into the snow. His chest heaved with his breath, and he lowered his mallet slowly, as though the action pained him as much as cutting off his own hand. His eyes were on Miri, and his expression said his heart was breaking for the second time.

Miri's own heart felt sore, like a burnt fingertip. She saw now that he would do whatever she needed—fight to dying, or lower his mallet, or even believe Peder's strange tale of quarry-speech spoken miles away. He had run through a snowstorm in the middle of the night to save his little girl.

She kicked backward at Dan and writhed to get free. It was like punching a stone. She hung limp from his hands and stared at her pa.

Everyone was quiet now. The frenzied running and brief fighting had stopped as quickly as it had begun. Miri and Dan stood in front of the academy steps. His hot, scratchy hands circled her throat, rubbing back and forth as if he rehearsed twisting her neck. Before her stood the wall of villagers.

She was comforted to see that many of the academy girls had made it behind the villagers, and they hugged one another and cried. The villagers had overwhelmed four bandits—three lay in the snow, a quarryman's boot on each of their backs, and a fourth squirmed as Frid's oldest brother held an iron lever across his neck. Miri wondered if any of the bandits were thinking of a mountain that could warn its people at the touch of an outsider's boot.

But the villagers held only four bandits, and the remaining eleven had seized some of the fleeing academy girls. Miri spotted Esa, Gerti, Katar, Britta, and Frid among the captive. Miri shivered. There was no window she could crawl through now.

The cold soaked further and further inside her like mold creeping through bread, and the minute of silent tension seemed hours. When Os spoke, the sound of his voice closed the space, making the outside night feel like a crowded room.

"We have four of your men, you have nine of our daughters. We make a nice, easy trade: you go on your way, and no one's blood melts the snow tonight."

Dan laughed. "Hardly a fair trade, quarryman. How about this—you keep the four men, give us back the other girls, and we send them home safe and sound once the prince pays."

There was a murmur of anger. Some of the villagers cursed at Dan and squeezed the shafts of their weapons. Os growled, his voice like the mountain rumbling.

"Not one of our daughters leaves our sight, and if even one is hurt, I make certain none of you leave this mountain with any limbs attached." Os's glance flicked to his daughter Gerti in the clutches of the one-eyed bandit. When his eyes returned to Dan, his expression said he would enjoy the chance to tear off a few limbs. "Let them come to us now and we'll release your four men and let you all go alive and running. That's a good offer. Don't dismiss it for your pride."

Dan spat into the snow. "I came here for some royal skin to ransom and I'm not leaving without—"

"You heard our terms," said Os. "Why don't you let what I've said roll around in your head before you decide to die tonight."

Dan did not answer immediately, and Miri wondered if Os would have more success using the principles of Diplomacy.

The snow kept falling between them, soft and light, the clumps of flakes sometimes rising and spinning on a gust. To Miri, the snowfall was strange and gentle. Everything else that night was hard and dangerous, like slabs of falling ice and windstorms that can blow people off cliffs. The weather did not recognize that at any moment Dan could crack her neck as if she were a rabbit fattened for the stew. Down the flakes came, slow and sweet as petals in a breeze.

Dan spat again, marking a small hole in the snow. The action said he had made a decision. "I want a prize for my trouble, and I will have it or this girl is first to go. I'm not jesting." His rough skin scratched her neck.

"Neither are we," said Miri's pa, his look set on Dan, rigid as stone, as though he were carved from the mountain itself.

"Come on, Dan." The bandit holding Katar spoke quietly enough that his voice would not carry to the villagers. "We had a good rest and ate our fill. We could just be done with it."

"Shut up, you idiot!" said Dan, and Miri gagged as his hold constricted. "I told you that you have to think bigger. We don't have what we came for, and we're not leaving without a princess to ransom."

"I am," said the bandit holding Gerti. He pushed her to the ground and backed away, his one eye darting as if trying to keep a watch on everything at once. "Something's not right on this mountain. It knew that we were here, told the villagers, just like the girls said. Next thing, the mountain will bury us alive and no one will cry, or those men will lop off my arms. I lost an eye for you once, Dan, and I'm not losing my arms, too."

Gerti ran to Os and gripped his leg. Miri could see the big man shudder with relief.

"You're talking like a fool," said Dan. Spit flew from his mouth as he spoke. "I order you to stay."

The one-eyed bandit looked over the men and women with levers and mallets clutched in both hands, looked up into the snowstorm, shuddered, and turned to leave. Several others pushed away their hostages and followed him.

"Dangerous place," one muttered.

Frid shoved down the two bandits who had been holding her. They seemed ready to fight back, but she held up her fists and gave them such a glare as to hope they would. They dusted the snow from their knees and caught up with the other deserters, looking back as they went as if afraid the mountain itself would follow.

"Get back here!" shouted Dan. "You leave now and you are no part of this band!"

The snow thickened, and in moments the departing bandits had disappeared behind the white screen. That seemed to make others nervous, and three more dropped their hostages and ran. Now only Onor and Dogface stood beside Dan.

"This one could be the princess," said Onor, shaking Esa. "I'm not shoving a girl worth one hundred horses into the snow."

Dogface held his one weapon, a dagger, to Britta's chest and idly flicked its tip against her shirt. A strand of cloth ripped. Miri struggled again, and Dan's hold tightened. If only she had a weapon. Snowflakes stuck to her eyelashes and tears of frustration blurred her vision so that she could not make out her father's face.

Miri knew Dan would never let her go, and he

would wring her neck before any mallet could reach him. Os was bargaining again, trying to make the remaining bandits see the futility of taking just three girls, but Miri felt no hesitation in her captor's hands.

Somewhere far above the snowfall, dawn appeared. The world gradually lightened, lifting the rose and peach hues from the air, making everything a clear silver. She began to see the villagers more plainly, the early light picking out the lines under their eyes and around their mouths, and she felt her heart swell so large that it almost hurt. There was Peder, his hands red with cold, no doubt having left too quickly to find his gloves. There was Doter's round face, Miri's pa as hard and square as a foundation stone, Frid's six brothers, and her ma bigger than any of them. Her family, her playmates, her protectors and neighbors and friends—those people were her world.

She realized with sudden clarity that she did not want to live far away from the village where Mount Eskel's shadow fell like a comforting arm. The mountain was home—the linder dust, the rhythm of the quarry, the chain of mountains, the people she knew as well as the feel of her own skin. And now, looking at them for perhaps the last time, she thought she loved them so much that her chest would burst before the bandit had time to kill her dead.

She had to chance something, and soon. To give herself courage, she put her hand in her skirt pocket and touched the linder hawk. Until that moment, she had forgotten it was there.

"I don't think we'll rest easy in this house anymore," Dan was saying. "Guess we'd better take our loot here and go." He started to back away from the villagers and toward the road that led down the mountain.

"Do you think we'll let you leave with those girls?" said Os. "We know they've little chance of survival in your hands."

"That's a chance you'll have to take," said Dan. "Because if you attack us now, I guarantee their survival prospects are much, much worse."

The villagers hefted their weapons and shifted their stance, but none advanced.

Dan kept walking backward, and Onor and Dogface followed. He seemed to be trying to find the road by feel, but the snow was stacked deep.

Miri knew the mountain. Even in the snowstorm she could see he was veering too far to his left. The cliff edge was getting closer. If only she could prod him closer still. As quiet as an exhale, she sang to herself, "No wolf falters before the bite. So strike. No hawk wavers before the dive. Just strike."

"Everyone stay still," said Dan. "We'll be gone soon, and you look for your girls come spring thaw. They'll be just fine."

She looked to her right and saw terror frozen on Britta's and Esa's faces like ice on a windowpane. To her left, the snow obscured the cliff's edge. She needed help to get him there.

Miri knew her pa loved her, knew that now with a peace like the mildest summer evening. She knew he would throw himself off the mountain to save her. But, as Doter said, he was a house with shutters closed. She could not trust that he would understand her quarry-speech plea.

Peder had heard her call from miles away. He would understand.

Miri struggled again, but this time with no hope of getting free. She just wanted a moment of contact with the ground, a chance to dig her foot into the snow and feel stone. The touch came, and she gripped the hawk in her pocket, hoping that bit of linder could help as well. With all the will inside her and quiet as the flakes falling, she sang out in quarry-speech.

The memory she chose was Peder falling into an unseen ice-melt hole and disappearing from view. She did not have to wonder long if he understood.

"Don't think we won't follow you," said Peder.

Snowflakes lay thick in his tawny curls, silver crowning gold. "We'll hound you as far as the sea if we have to."

Some of the adults frowned at his outburst, but Peder did not take his eyes from Miri and Dan. He prodded Jans and Almond, Bena's older brother, and they followed him away from the line of villagers to the left of the three bandits. Miri felt Dan shift.

"Not so close, little kitten," said Dan. "I'm a thief and a murderer, remember? You can't trust me not to kill her out of spite."

Peder and the others slowed, but they kept advancing to Dan's right, forcing him to change his path just a little. Miri thought it was enough. She concentrated on keeping her body relaxed, not stiffening in anticipation, giving Dan no indication of what she was about to try.

Don't hesitate. Just swing. Miri grabbed the linder hawk from her pocket, held it like a dagger, and stabbed Dan's wrist with the sharpened tip of an outstretched wing.

Dan hollered and let go. Miri dropped to the ground, rolled away from him, and crawled through the snow. The shock of pain lasted only a moment, and he yelled and leaped after her.

But there was the edge. Miri did not have time to

be careful. Hoping she had judged her position correctly, she rolled over the cliff and reached for the rocky shelf where she and Katar had talked the day of the exam.

She hit earth, but the relief filling her chest was stopped by the sickening feeling of her feet sliding off the ledge. Her hands scrambled for a hold and found the hanging roots of a cliff tree. She looked up to see Dan step over the edge, his face wide with surprise to find no ground beneath his feet. He fell.

Miri's body shook with a hard yank. Dan had one hand on the cliff, another on her ankle.

The wood creaked in her hands. The root slid from its hold in the ledge like a snake through water, then jerked to a stop. Below, Dan clenched her leg, and farther down, the snow kept falling, falling, so far that she could not see a flake come to rest at the bottom. The falling snow made the cliff seem to run on forever, like a river stretching out to the faraway sea.

Her hands were on fire, her leg was numb. She tried to kick him off but could not budge his weight. Dan tried to climb the cliff wall with one hand, using her leg to pull himself up. Miri screamed from the pain of holding on. Her hands were slipping, and she felt herself nearly falling with the snow.

Then something struck Dan on the forehead. He

looked up, but his eyes seemed blind, as if his vision were lost trying to follow a snowflake. His hold on the cliff slipped, his weight lessened, and then, unexpectedly, Miri was watching him get smaller and smaller. His arms and legs splayed as though he were making a snow angel in midair. The wind blew the falling snow into circles and spirals, washing out everything below, so that Miri did not see him hit the ground.

She looked up. Her pa was leaning over the cliff edge, the mallet gone from his hand.

Chapter Twenty-four

Night is calling, Away, come away!
Empty your mind of troubles and dreams
Empty your heart of all daylight things
Night is calling, Forget! But the day
Will not wait, not long now, won't delay

Miri was only hazily aware of what happened after Dan fell. She managed to keep her grip on the root until someone pulled her onto firm, snowy ground. For a moment she thought Peder was near, and she smelled the dry sweetness of Doter's clothes soap. Then she disappeared into her father's huge, warm embrace.

She did not let go of her pa for hours, watching from his arms as Onor and Dogface released Britta and Esa and with the other four bandits fled the academy. Twenty stout quarrymen followed briefly to make certain they kept going. Esa was with Peder and their parents, their ma attacking her with breathless kisses. Britta's relatives patted her back. Liana approached

Miri and whispered in her ear, "I should've voted for you for academy princess," and when Bena caught Miri's eye, the older girl did not glare.

A few men stood guard around the academy in case any bandits had the gall to return, and the rest took shelter inside from the snow.

Miri remembered Knut and Olana, and they were released from their locked closet, cold and underfed. Frid's ma took care of Knut's broken arm, and Olana stood by as if anxious to help and kept repeating, "Thank you, yes, thank you."

It was full morning, but they had been up all night, so they stoked the fire in the bedchamber and lay down to rest until afternoon. Families piled together on one pallet, made pillows of one another's chests and legs, and held on for warmth and just for joy that everyone was all right. Miri snuggled under the scoop of her pa's arm, his heat spreading over her like the thickest blanket. She pulled Britta to her other side, and they slept with their arms entwined.

After all woke and felt their stomachs grumble, a few women conducted an inventory of the food supply and returned to report that no one would be living at the academy that winter. The bandits had eaten and let rot a village year's worth of meat in just a few days.

The remaining food was enough for one group meal of flat bread and porridge with a few strips of meat to fry.

It was eerie to step out of the academy that afternoon and into blazing sunshine. Heaps of snow lay at their feet, smoothed by a breeze and, under that sun, more brilliant than polished linder. Miri wrapped her arms around her chest and observed how the snow had kept falling for days, then stopped at just the right time. When she thought about it with her head only, she did not believe that the mountain could really hear her, but her heart wished it to be so. Just in case, she whispered, "Thank you," and blew a subtle kiss to that white peak against the sunny blue sky.

Though the trek was precarious and slow going through the deep snow, the mood was as merry as a holiday. The first time Miri slipped into a pit and met snow up to her elbows, her father lifted her onto his shoulders. At such a moment, she decided that she did not mind being so small. She looked back and spotted the tip of an academy chimney before it disappeared, and wondered when they would return. But she did not worry much about it. Her thoughts were filling with the lush expectations of a quarry filled with snow, allowing everyone days of free time, of Marda and reading lessons, of winter at home with plenty of fuel and plenty of food.

Up ahead, she heard Olana and Doter talking.

"But what will I do for weeks and weeks?" asked Olana.

"Don't worry, my dear," said Doter, who had heard reports of the tutor from her daughter. "We'll put you to work."

Olana stayed with Esa's family that winter, a fact that earned Esa many sympathetic shakes of the head and a few smug grins. But it was not long before Olana proved she could be useful skinning rabbits and was dispatched to many houses to perform the unpleasant task. Knut stayed with Gerti's family and any night could be heard laughing heartily with Os, who took to the all-work man like a lost brother.

Miri insisted Britta stay with her, and among the three girls the housework was done before noon, leaving plenty of time to help Marda with her studies. A few older girls started to drift in whenever Miri was teaching, then three of Frid's brothers, and one of Gerti's little sisters followed, until Miri's house was full to bursting every afternoon. Sometimes Peder came too. Things felt oddly uneasy between them, askew, expectant. She waited for him to speak first, and he did not.

The night after Gerti's sister read her first page, Miri told Marda, "This is what I want. I've been all muddled and stirred up by the princess stuff, but now I know. We'll need a bigger building so we can invite all the boys to come learn to read. And we need real books, and clay tablets like the academy has. And maybe we could sell the linder from the academy floor so the quarry could spare all the men and women for a day or two a week and the entire village can learn!"

Marda shook her head. "You'd teach the goats their letters if they'd stand still for it."

One afternoon while boiling the laundry, Miri proposed the idea of a village academy to Britta, Esa, and Frid.

"I'm tired of books and letters and such," said Frid. "But my brothers are curious to learn reading at least, though they said they didn't see much value in the other subjects we studied."

"Your brother Lew swore to me that he was dying to study Poise," said Miri, trying not to smile.

"Yes, he's got a fine curtsy," answered Frid with an equally straight face.

"Well, I feel like I could keep learning forever." Esa pulled one of her mother's smocks out of the pot with a stick. "I'd like my ma to be able to join our village academy, too. I used to think she was the smartest person in the world, and I don't like knowing more than she does, about the world beyond Mount Eskel anyway."

"If we're going to be teachers, then we'd better learn all we can," said Miri.

Olana was anxious to be spared village chores and teach again, so the academy girls agreed to pack themselves into the small chapel most afternoons, granted they could bring Marda and any other sisters who so desired as well as pick the subjects taught. No more Poise and Conversation—instead they deluged her with questions. Olana seemed to know when she was beaten.

Miri wanted to learn more about Mathematics to help with trading, Liana's interests tended toward etiquette at court, and Esa was curious about the social classes beyond the mountain.

When Katar inquired about a princess's daily duties, Olana detailed the responsibilities of the current queen of Danland—overseeing the administration of the palace and servants, paying calls with delegates and courtiers, planning celebrations, maintaining friendly relations with the merchants and traders of neighboring kingdoms, a day as long as any quarrier's.

That afternoon when class was over, many of the original academy girls remained in the chapel. It seemed they all had the same question spinning inside.

"Do you want to be the princess?" Esa asked Frid.

"No. I like working in the quarry."

"Sometimes I want to," said Esa. "I used to want it more, and the prince was nice enough. But things are getting better here, and I don't want to leave my family or make them leave the mountain."

Gerti was sitting on the floor, her arms around her knees. "You know Olana's book of tales? There's a story in it about a girl who meets a prince and falls in love with him on the spot, and all her dreams come true when he pulls her onto his horse and they ride off to the palace. I thought when I met him it might be like that." Gerti shrugged. "Steffan was pretty nice, I guess, but . . ." She shrugged again.

"I want to," said Liana. "I want to wear ball gowns and live in a palace."

Miri frowned. Liana did look as lovely as Miri imagined a princess should, but she thought Steffan deserved better.

Several other girls admitted proudly or shyly that they, too, still hoped to be the princess. Tonna had even begun to wear her hair twisted up all the time.

"Didn't you hear Olana?" said Bena, apparently angry that Liana disagreed with her yet again. "It won't be one long ball. It'll be boring work, long days talking to people you don't care about, and married to a dull boy with a fancy title. I can't believe after all our lessons in History, knowing about all the assassinations and political plots and wars and barren queens, that anyone would want to be a princess."

"Well, I do," said Liana. "My reign would be different. It would be fun."

Katar looked at Miri for the briefest moment but did not voice her opinion. Miri knew Katar did not care about the work or the gowns, loving Steffan, or missing home. She simply wanted to be chosen and given the chance to leave.

"Do you want to, Miri?" asked Britta.

Miri blew out her lips. There was no hearth in the chapel, and she watched her breath turn white against the cold air. She wanted to form a village academy and feel at home on the mountain, she wanted to be with her pa and Marda, and she thought she wanted to be with Peder. If that was what he wanted. She knew those things, yet she could not let go of the idea of being a princess, not after all the hoping and wondering. So she said, "It seems strange to still think about this, after the bandits and everything. It seems like the world has changed and we shouldn't still be talking about things like marrying a prince."

"Whether we want to or not," said Esa, "if he chooses us, would we be able to refuse?"

After months of bowing to their desires, Olana dug in her heels and insisted on reviewing some princess subjects. "My purpose is to ready you for the prince's next visit, and at the very least we must rehearse our curtsies and dances."

"Tutor Olana," said Miri, "it doesn't seem very effective to keep dancing by ourselves. Some of the village boys might be willing to learn the dances and practice with us."

So when spring holiday again lit the mountain with bonfires and music, the village enjoyed its first ball. Miri wore her chapel skirt and her hair loose and smiled at Peder when the drums and yipper began playing. That night he was not the distant, uncertain boy who sometimes passed by without a word—that night he was Peder, her best friend. He asked her for the first dance.

The lowlander dances did not separate partners with a ribbon, and Miri found herself holding Peder's hand for the first time since they were tiny children. He pressed his fingers against her lower back and led her through a promenade, and they conversed so easily that Miri laughed to remember her awkward exchanges with Steffan.

The talking hushed when they moved through the positions of "Lady of Water," a short dance that required partners to face each other, their palms pressed together, their faces just a breath apart. Peder swallowed and looked at his feet and over her head. But midway through the dance, he relaxed and met her eyes.

Miri's heart buzzed. She wished she could say something just right. The future loomed before her, and she felt as though the prince stood between them, keeping them one step apart.

"What are you thinking?" asked Peder.

"I was thinking of the prince, when he comes back . . . ," she said, then wished she had not. Peder's smile was gone.

"Are you angry?" Miri whispered, and he shrugged. When the drum and yipper stopped playing, Peder walked away.

"He thinks you want to marry the prince," said Britta at her side.

"I know," said Miri. She instinctively put her hand in her pocket, but she had lost the linder hawk down the cliff.

The matter of the princess still felt unsettled inside her, a silty streambed that shifts underfoot. She did not understand why Steffan had left, but he had liked her best. He had said so. If he returned and asked her to go with him to Asland, to be a princess, to give her family that house in the painting, how could she say no? Steffan was nice. Miri could imagine becoming friends, even dear friends. She would find ways to make him laugh, and he would show her all of Danland. And perhaps she would be happy.

But the nearer his return, the tighter Miri felt herself clinging to Mount Eskel as she had to that tree root on the cliff. The mountain was home. Her pa was home. And Peder . . . She allowed herself to hope for Peder. Her wishes were too big for a hillside of miri flowers.

Chapter Twenty-five

Plumb line is swinging
Spring hawk is winging
Eskel is singing

The first morning that dawned free of frost, Miri and Britta sat on the large boulder beside Miri's house, watching the west road.

"I'm so tired of waiting and wondering," said Miri. "I want to do something new. I wish I could teach you quarry-speech."

"You're in a mood lately to teach everything," said Britta. "I'll bet I haven't been up here long enough to get drenched in linder, but there might be something I can help you do. You once said lowlanders were supposed to be good with gardens." The corners of her eyes crinkled with her smile.

They cleared some ground of rubble rock until their nails were chipped and fingers sore. Britta showed her how to loosen the soil and make furrows in the earth to catch water runoff. She dipped her finger into the dirt and plopped in a seed.

"This will be a pea vine, if it has a chance to grow."

Miri had never eaten a fresh pea, and Britta said they tasted like a spring morning. They planted the rest of the seeds Britta had brought from the lowlands and talked about the fresh things they would eat all summer. Neither of them mentioned that the prince would come soon and someone would not be there to eat squash and cherry tomatoes.

That afternoon, the pounding in the quarry paused at the sound of trumpets.

"Prince Steffan of Danland returned last night to the princess's academy!" shouted a messenger from the bed of a wagon. "All academy girls are requested to attend him this day."

Miri and Britta readied themselves, taking extra care to wash their faces and comb their hair.

"Who do you think he'll pick?" asked Miri.

Britta just shrugged. She seemed too nervous to speak.

Miri's father watched them in silence, and Marda brushed off the tabletop again and again. Miri knew they were not anxious for a house in the lowlands with a beautiful garden or clothing made from expensive cloth or silver forks for their food. They just wanted Miri home again soon. Miri paused to feel the goodness of that thought—her pa wanted her home. She believed that now, and it made her feel as if she were still wearing the silver gown.

After the bandit attack, the parents would not let their daughters far from sight, so thirty quarry workers accompanied the academy girls. The girls scarcely spoke, and no one laughed or skipped or hurled stones over the cliff's edge. Miri walked with Britta, Esa, and Frid, and after a moment Britta managed to catch Katar's hand as well.

"And we'll all still be friends," said Miri, "no matter who is princess."

They all agreed. Britta only nodded. Miri wondered if Britta might be sick again.

Word of the bandits must have reached the capital, as the academy was surrounded by soldiers. The quarriers joined them.

Inside the academy there were no tapestries or chandeliers, no wardrobe of gowns. One woman in a neat, green dress greeted them at the door and led them into the nearly bare dining hall. Miri tried to flatten a crumple in her wool shirt and noticed other girls arranging their clothing or smoothing down loose hairs.

"Prince Steffan will attend you in just a few minutes," said the woman. "Please wait here."

"I don't understand," Esa whispered to the girls near her. "If we're not going to dance and curtsy and converse again, why didn't he choose someone before?"

Frid shrugged. "Maybe he was too cold to think straight. My grandfather gets soggy-brained in the winter."

"Or maybe you shouldn't have arm-wrestled him, Frid," Miri whispered back. "The first rule of Poise states, 'Never pick up your dance partner and toss him across the floor.'"

"Oh, I can't, I just can't," Britta said suddenly, and ran out.

Miri glanced at the doorway where the prince would enter, but she did not hesitate to follow after Britta.

Britta dashed down the academy steps and plopped herself behind a large boulder.

"What's happened?" Miri sat beside her. "You look sick again, Britta. Do you want me to fetch Knut?"

Britta shook her head. She sucked her bottom lip as if desperate to keep herself from crying.

"What is it?" asked Miri.

Britta plucked at her clothes, rubbed her forehead, tugged her ear, and seemed overwhelmed by agitation. "I can't see the prince. I can't let him see me! I know him."

Miri blinked. "You know the prince?"

Britta whimpered and put her face in her hands. Her voice came out muffled. "I hate this, Miri. I should've told you before, but whenever I thought about it I felt so ill and embarrassed and horrified and—"

"You know the prince."

Britta nodded. "My father wasn't a merchant. He was . . . is . . . a nobleman. And I grew up with Steffan, with the prince, at least for part of each year, because he would summer in an estate near my home, and he was adventuresome and kind, and all the other boys were so stuffy, so he said he liked to be with me. We used to play this game where we were poor folk who could eat only what we could find, and we'd scavenge the gardens for anything edible—green tomatoes, berries, pansy flowers. We'd dig up baby carrots and eat them unwashed as though we were starving."

Britta stopped and looked at Miri with concern in her mild brown eyes. "I wonder if that seems rude to you, Steffan and I playing at being starved."

"No," said Miri. "I guess your life was very different then."

Britta nodded. "It was different—not better than here, not worse. I haven't missed any of it really, except not feeling so cold in the winter and not being hungry. And I haven't missed anybody much, except Steffan." She sighed and put her hands over her eyes. "My father had hoped we'd wed. Whenever Father talked about it I just wanted to curl up and hide, but I did dream. . . . Steffan never said anything, and of course I never had a real chance because the priests choose where the princess will be found. But when I was old enough to think about it, I'd hoped he . . . hoped that . . ."

"That he loved you back."

Britta looked up. Her eyes were glassy. "If you knew my father, you would probably tremble to imagine his reaction when he heard the priests' divination named a place where he owned no land, far away from any of his friends or connections. I certainly hid from him for a week. That was a bad time." Britta shuddered. "But he refused to give up. He somehow discovered the name of a family on Mount Eskel and sent me on a trader's wagon with an order to claim that he was dead and that I was related to the family. Then his daughter really would be a girl who lived on Mount Eskel."

"And so you are," said Miri quietly.

"I'm so sorry, Miri. You must think I've been such a liar. I was mortified that my family had such ridiculous hopes, and I thought you'd hate me for being a rich lowlander, or just for being so foolish. In truth, I was a little glad to come up here. I've long believed my parents cared about me only if I could tie them to the throne."

"You really are Lady Britta."

"Please don't call me that!"

Miri frowned. "But if you knew that the prince would choose you . . ."

"But he won't!" Britta leapt to her feet and paced around the stones. "For a year, I've been terrified of the day Steffan arrived, and he'd see me pretending to be a Mount Eskel girl, and he'd say, 'What are you doing here?' And I'd say, 'I came chasing after you because I want to marry you. . . .' Aah! Can you imagine, Miri? He'll detest me then, or laugh in my face, or pretend he doesn't know me."

"And if he doesn't detest you or laugh or—"

"No, don't say that. I have to believe it won't happen. Whenever I try to hope, it hurts so much. For months, it seemed no one here liked me a whit, and all I had to look forward to was making a fool of myself in front of the boy I've been in love with for years. And then when I got to know all the girls at the academy, and I realized how much smarter and prettier you all are than I am, his choice seemed obvious."

"You know him, and you really think he'd choose me over you?"

Britta stopped pacing. "Of course. You're the smartest person I've ever known, and a year ago you couldn't even read. You're clever and funny—why wouldn't anyone want to marry you? I want you to know that I've been preparing myself all year for the time when he doesn't pick me. It'll hurt, a little, but I really will be happy when it's you."

"I . . ." Could he really? Miri looked out to the chain of mountains, blue, purple, gray, and glanced over her shoulder to the tip of the road that led home. The dream of the house with the garden felt like candle smoke—shifting, lovely, but almost gone. "I don't want to be the princess."

"Miri," said Britta, sounding exasperated.

"I don't. I really don't. What a relief to know that now! It wouldn't be fair, Britta. Like you said once, the princess should be someone who would be really, really happy. Someone who loves Steffan."

"Miri! Britta!" Esa called from the steps of the academy. "Are you out here? Olana said to find you. The prince is about to come see us."

Britta put a hand to her stomach and groaned. "I

can't do it, Miri. I think I might actually die."

Miri laughed, and laughing felt like precisely the best thing to do. She pulled Britta to her feet and hugged her hard.

"What's so funny?" asked Britta, starting to smile just at the sound of Miri's laugh.

"You are. Britta, you survived Olana, Katar, two mountain winters, and a wolf pack of bandits. You might throw up, but you won't die now. Though if you're going to throw up, do it here. It'll be a tad more embarrassing in the middle of your curtsy."

Britta's face went ashen. "Do you think I might . . . ?"

Miri laughed again and tugged her arms. "Come on, let's go see your prince."

They rushed into the dining hall just as Steffan emerged from the far door. His eyes scanned the room expectantly, and when they stopped on Britta, he took a half step backward. He smiled, then he smiled larger, then he grinned. His shoulders relaxed, and Miri half expected him to do something boyish and outrageous, like leap for joy or gallop to her side. Instead, he bowed, grand and low.

Steffan broke his gaze from Britta and walked around the room, nodding at each girl. When he came to Britta, he stopped. Miri never would have believed it possible, but all his careful poise vanished. He bobbed up and down on the balls of his feet.

"Good afternoon to you, miss. I don't believe we were introduced at my last visit."

"My name is Britta, Your Highness," she said with a perfect curtsy, though her voice caught a little. "Britta Paweldaughter."

"It is my pleasure to meet you, Britta Paweldaughter." The prince bowed, took her hand, and kissed it. With his mouth over her hand, he said softly, "I'm Steffan."

"A pleasure, sir. Steffan." Her face could not bear the solemnity. She smiled with such ardor that Miri's own heart beat faster just to see her.

Steffan continued on, greeting the rest of the girls, then conversed quietly with the woman in the green dress. She nodded and motioned a priest in from the corridor. In his dark brown shirt and white cap, the priest reminded Miri of Mount Eskel's peak in early spring.

"Prince Steffan, heir to the throne of Danland, has selected his chosen princess," said the woman. "Britta Paweldaughter, please come forward."

Britta began to shake even harder, and her ruddy cheeks all but drained of color. Miri was afraid she might fall over or faint, and she put her arm around her and walked her across the room. Steffan rushed forward and took her other arm.

"Are you all right, Britta?" he whispered. "Do you need to sit down?"

Britta shook her head. Miri waited to one side as Britta and Steffan stood before the priest.

"I choose Britta Paweldaughter as betrothed to the throne," said Steffan.

"And does she accept?" the priest asked.

"I accept Steffan Sabetson as my betrothed." Britta took a deep breath, as if she had been holding it for a long time.

The priest spoke a lengthy discourse for the ritual of betrothal binding, including naming all the kings and queens from King Dan on down. Miri noticed that he missed one in the middle, and she tilted her head and looked back at the girls. Others had apparently noticed, too, and tittered about it. The priest stopped, corrected himself, and continued on.

Olana, watching from the corridor, smiled proudly.

When the ceremony ended, the priest turned to face all the girls. "The king wishes me to convey his approval of this academy and of each of you. In honor of his son's betrothed and this academy, the king renews his love for Mount Eskel and raises its status from a territory to the sixteenth province of Danland.

Let the potentials approach." No one moved, so the priest gestured to the academy girls. "You are the potentials."

The girls stepped forward in a nice, even line, and Miri joined them.

"I name each of you graduates of this academy, citizens of Danland, and ladies of the princess."

"What does that mean?" asked Frid, staring wide-eyed at the priest.

"At the very least," said Steffan, "it means you are all invited to Asland to attend our wedding in one year's time."

The girls exclaimed and turned to one another, chattering about seeing the things they had learned about, and the food and dances.

"The ocean!" said Esa. "We'll see the ocean."

Katar stood alone, a polite smile frozen on her face. Miri wondered if she was thinking not of going to the capital, but of having to come back again.

The prince's party set out a splendid luncheon of cold meats, cheeses, fruits, and breads, and they all sat at the academy benches, planning their trip to the lowlands. Miri watched Britta beside the boy she loved. Her eyes shone, her smile was wide and genuine. Her gestures lost their flustered anxiousness and became smooth and confident, the weight of her insecurity lifted.

Miri's heart was warm and her lips kept insisting on a smile, but for some reason she could not eat as heartily as she would like. She wondered if she might be jealous that she was not chosen. No, that thought rang false. She observed Britta and Steffan, the way they leaned toward each other, the way no one else seemed near.

Miri's heart throbbed. It must be a marvelous thing to feel so sure, to be able to meet someone's eyes and not look away.

"Don't go home yet," Britta said to Miri as the priest summoned her and Steffan out of the room.

So when Esa and most of the other girls left for the village, Miri stayed behind. She walked the academy corridors, eyeing the floorstones and calculating which areas would be the easiest to pull up to sell without damaging the building. She even peeked into the now empty closet and hissed at the dark, "I'm not afraid of you, you tiny rat! I'm a mountain girl."

Perhaps an hour later, she spotted Britta and Steffan walking together outside. Steffan held Britta's arm in his own, and they talked low, having to incline their heads close to hear. Their foreheads nearly touched, their hair mingling. A hawk passed overhead, and when Britta and Steffan looked up at its curling dive, Britta caught sight of Miri and motioned for her to join them.

"There you are!" said Britta. "Miri Larendaughter, may I present Steffan."

"We've met," said Miri, making a proper curtsy, "the night you were sick."

"Britta, is that why you weren't at the ball?"

Britta nodded. "I was barely conscious. I think I was just terrified that you'd consider me foolish for being here and choose someone else anyway."

Steffan laughed, making eyes with Miri to share the joke. "Britta, I *knew* you were here! Your father sent word, and I was so relieved, because then you and I . . ."

He stopped, and this time both he and Britta blushed, finding the topic of their marriage still new and awkward.

"So," Steffan continued, his eyes down, "when I thought you weren't here after all, I was so disappointed I couldn't hide it, and I tried to meet all the girls and still make a choice, but I'm afraid I did a poor job of it." He glanced at Miri.

"He did a stunning impression of a stone column," said Miri.

"You didn't retreat into your stiff, formal self, did you, Steffan?"

"I was nervous! You weren't here, and I hadn't prepared myself to meet anyone else."

"I would have laughed if I'd seen you," said Britta.

"Not to worry, because Miri did for you. I could have guessed that she of all the girls would be your friend. I am sorry for leaving the academy so abruptly, but I couldn't make a decision until I knew what had happened with Britta. You can imagine my frustration when I returned to the capital and learned from one of the servants that there had been an academy girl who hadn't attended the ball, and then have snow seal the mountain pass and have to wait all this time . . . Well, it was a long winter.

"I spent more of it than I should have liked locked in a small room with the chief priest going over books of law. I wanted to be certain there would be no obstacle to our betrothal, so I told him of you, that your parents were not from Mount Eskel and still living. It took a couple of months, but eventually he agreed that no law could prevent it. I have the impression, though, that the priests might amend that rule before our . . . before the next prince heir marries."

Steffan was loath to leave Britta's side, but a minister soon had him rounded up to speak with Olana and sign official documents.

"I'll be right back," he said several times, turning

around as he walked away to wave at Britta.

Britta waved back and put a hand on her chest. "I feel like my heart will burst. How could everything be so wonderful?"

"You deserve it," said Miri.

"I can think of one thing that would make it nicer." Britta smiled, as though with a secret. "You remember what we learned about the difference between a territory and a province."

"Oh," said Miri, the thought stirring her. "Mount Eskel will need a delegate to represent us at court."

"Your status as an academy graduate and princess's lady makes you a worthy candidate, and I know Steffan would be eager to recommend you to the chief delegate. Then for the majority of each year you could live in Asland with me!"

The offer was rich and inviting, an answer to miri flower wishes, but she hesitated only a moment before saying, "Take Katar instead."

"Katar? But why—"

"She's only a horror because she's so miserable. She'll be an excellent delegate, I really think she will. And I'd like to be home for a while."

"All right, but I'd rather be with you." Britta saw Steffan across the way, and she waved and sighed. "When you come to the wedding next spring, you'll have a chance to see Asland and decide if you want to stay. You could live in the palace as a princess's lady, or attend the university and become a tutor, or just sit in the palace library and read the year through. Be warned before you come that I plan on doing my best to keep you there."

"I hope so. I would like to see more of the world." Miri spotted the white cap and brown shirt of the priest as he stood near the cliff edge, gazing at the view. "I can't help wonder about the princess choosing—I mean, if you were destined to be the princess, why didn't the priests divine your own town Lonway instead of Mount Eskel?"

Britta glanced at the building. "Maybe the priests did know what they were doing. Maybe Mount Eskel didn't need a princess, just an academy."

The rest of the girls were heading back to the village, and they waved to Britta as they passed, shouting congratulations. Katar was among them, gazing at the ground as she walked.

"Katar, wait!" said Britta, running after her.

Miri watched as Britta offered the invitation. Katar's expression changed, quick as the end of a summer storm. Her old tightness relaxed, her chin started to quiver, and she turned her face away. Miri knew it must pain Katar to show such emotion, and she hoped

Britta would pretend not to notice or leave her alone. But instead, Britta embraced her.

Miri nodded, feeling confident that there was no one better in the world to be Katar's first friend.

The royal party was hitching horses to carriages and wagons, so Miri ran back into the academy with hopes of some last business. She had one gold coin in her pocket, a gift from her father, and she meant to use it well.

"I'd like to keep the clay tablets and some of the books," she said as she entered the classroom.

Olana was setting the last book in a leather sack. "I kept our agreement. Britta will recommend me to the prince for good work in the capital, so you have nothing to hold over me. You can have the tablets, but these books are from my personal collection, and you don't have anything of worth to trade."

Miri tossed her father's fat gold coin onto Olana's table. It clanged and rolled to a stop.

Olana scooped it off the table, and it disappeared into her pouch. "I was mistaken. Six of the books are yours to keep. You certainly excelled in Commerce."

Miri suspected Olana was being generous, but she did not argue. She selected six books and hugged them to her chest. They felt like the most valuable things in the world, better than a little gold coin, better than a wagon full of linder. Reading those books had changed her, and she could not wait to let the whole village feel that difference.

She wondered if she should say good-bye to Olana before leaving, but it seemed awkward, something a friend would say to a friend. So she walked to the door without a word.

"A moment, Miri."

Miri stopped. Olana was holding the painting of the house.

"Tell the other girls that I . . . You might explain how the burden of turning rough mountain girls into princesses, on my shoulders alone . . ." Her voice tightened, but if she was near tears, her eyes did not show it. She shook her head, and her familiar stern expression took hold of her features. "I had to provoke you, you know. I had to make you angry so you would want to study harder, to spite me. I don't regret any cruelty. It worked. But I do regret one lie." She hefted the painting. "There never was such a house. I brought this painting to give you girls another incentive to be diligent."

Miri had thought nothing could surprise her after learning the truth about Britta, but once again that day she found herself reeling with shock. Hours she had spent staring at that painting, imagining Pa and Marda walking through the garden, passing through its door, lounging in comfortable chairs by its hearth.

"But how would you get away with such a lie?"

"It doesn't really matter now, does it? Apparently Britta's family already has an estate much grander than the house in this painting. If the prince had chosen one of you girls, I doubted the royal ministers had any intention of bringing her family to the capital. No use getting angry over what-ifs." Olana placed the painting in an empty cloth sack and handed it to Miri. "Here. You're academy princess. You earned the painting."

Miri carefully added her books and tablets to the sack. A gift from anyone was a nice thing, but from Olana it felt like a miracle. And now she had something she could give her family. It was not a real house. It did not mean they could sit all day and watch the flowers grow. But Pa would have been bored, and Marda would have missed the mountain. Miri could still give them something beautiful, and they would never have to leave home. The painting was the best present after all.

"Thank you," said Miri, and meant it for more than just the painting. She left without another word, thinking that "thank you" was nicer than "good-bye" anyway.

After a final farewell to Knut, Britta, and Steffan,

Miri began her walk home, the precious sack cradled in her arms. She was watching the ground before her so she would not stumble and did not know someone had approached until she felt a tug on her sack.

Miri was startled, thinking of bandits, but it was Peder.

"Hello," he said, taking the bundle from her.

"Peder, I nearly lost my heart with surprise . . ." She looked away, afraid that mentioning her heart to Peder was too revealing.

"I thought I could walk you back. Esa returned hours ago and told me about Britta. I came to tell you, I'm glad you weren't chosen."

"Yes, so am I."

Peder exhaled loudly. "I was worried. It seemed these last months that you had been hoping . . . Are you really all right?"

Miri smiled. "Yes, I'm perfect."

Peder returned his mischievous smile. "That's what I've been thinking all along."

They walked in silence for a time, neither able to think of anything to say after that. Finally Peder spoke again and told her that his father had agreed that Peder could take the time to chisel designs into one block of linder.

"If any traders are interested," said Peder, "if they

will pay more for it than for a plain linder block, he says I might do it all the time. I don't think he ever would've given me the chance if things weren't so much better now. Thank you."

Miri had an impulse to laugh or say something funny or mocking, but instead she said, "You're welcome, Peder." Then she did laugh for no reason, her heart beating and her stomach all twisty feeling.

"What?" said Peder. "What's the joke?"

"No joke. I just feel good, good like laughing. Next year I'll go to the capital for the wedding, and you could go as well. You can study with stone artisans, and I can read all the books in the palace library."

"What if there are a hundred? Or a thousand?"

Miri balked at the thought. "There couldn't be that many in all the world. . . ." She tried to imagine it. Could there be? And how long would it take to read them? And what would they say?

"If you're going to read a thousand books, you should get started soon," said Peder.

"Maybe. But I haven't enjoyed home in so long, and now I think I can—I want to try. I want to make my pa's breakfast, and take care of Britta's garden, and spare Marda the slaying of the winter rabbits. And I want to open an academy in the village where anyone can come learn. Esa is going to help me."

"I think she'll enjoy that," said Peder.

"I've thought about it, and I decided that you can be a student, too, if you're good."

"Oh, really?"

"Yes, I suppose so," she said with an exaggerated sigh. "But it will cost you something—one linder hawk."

Peder nodded as if impressed. "An interesting choice of payment. What ever made you think of such a thing?"

"I had one before, and it was the most . . . Well, actually, the most precious thing I own is the week right after I was born when my mother held me and never put me down. But the hawk was the second most precious thing. I was sorry to lose it, and if you make me another one, I promise not to get taken captive by bandits and have to use it to save my life."

Instead of laughing, Peder hefted the sack and swallowed, looking very nervous. "Of course, I will, but I was wondering something else, if we, if you . . ."

Peder shook his head as if giving up on words, reached out, and took her hand. Miri bit her lip to keep herself from pulling away. She was certain he could feel her heartbeat in her fingers and would know that inside she was trembling and sighing. Then after a time she stopped worrying. She could feel his heartbeat, too, and it was as fast as a fleeing hare.

When they entered the village, Peder still kept hold of her hand. Frid stared as they passed, Esa blushed for them, Gerti and her three younger sisters giggled and chased after, chanting about a kiss for every miri petal. Twice Miri relaxed her hand in case he wanted to leave her, but he held on even tighter.

Only when they reached her house did he finally let go. "We can talk later, or go for a walk tonight, if you like."

Marda and Pa were back from the quarry early and sitting on the large stones beside Britta's garden. Miri gave them the painting, leaned her head against her pa's shoulder, and smiled as they cooed over the gift.

They watched the light change in the west, striking the afternoon with yellows and oranges, and sang a harmony of three parts. Pa sang low, Marda high, and Miri the melody. "Plumb line is swinging, spring hawk is winging, Eskel is singing."

At their feet, the curly fronds poking up in Britta's garden were greener than the mountain grass, greener than the needles on the small, twisted trees, almost greener than the garden in the painting. Miri thought if she could just keep the goats out of it, Britta's garden would grow to be the greenest thing she would ever see.

She leaned over the little rock fence to pick fallen linder chips from among the plants and tossed them up the slope of scree. Among the gray scraps of rubble rock, the white and silver linder gleamed like jewels. From the cracks in the rocks all around, the miri flowers were already blooming.

Literature Circle Questions

Use these questions and the activities that follow to enhance your experience of reading *Princess Academy* by Shannon Hale.

1. What are the origins of Miri's name?

2. Why does Miri work at home but Marda works in the quarry?

3. Why does Miri think Britta lies to Tutor Olana about not knowing how to read?

4. Describe the setting of the story. What are some key words that help to show the type of community it takes place in?

5. Early on, it is obvious that Miri is a special person. How do we know that? What are some examples of her character and wit?

6. How does learning to read affect Miri—and the other girls around her?

7. Miri learns about quarry-speech throughout the course of the story. What is quarry-speech? Why is it so important to the community? And why is it so important to the events of the story?

8. Miri says of the mountain and its many secrets, "I'll figure you out" (p. 90). What is she looking to discover?

9. Miri discovers a new and different type of intelligence as she and her classmates study together. She tells Marda, "You're smart" (p. 150). How does Miri define smart at this point in the story? How does her understanding of the word change as the story goes on?

10. After leaving the academy, the girls approach Tutor Olana with a list of terms that she must accept upon their return. What are the steps the girls have learned to take to convince Tutor Olana? When you want to convince someone to do something, what do you do?

11. Esa says, "Katar's a thornbush protecting a hare that's too skinny to eat" (p. 157). What does she mean? What type of person is Katar, and what do we learn about her past that makes her actions more understandable?

12. Miri helps her father—and all of the residents of Mount Eskel—understand that the lowlanders are taking advantage of their low prices for linder. Why is Miri nervous to talk to the town about this?

13. Miri, Katar, and Britta are very different girls. How do they compare with each other? Create a chart, listing the things that make them similar and different.

14. Pa is described to Miri as "a house with shutters closed" (p. 176). What do you think that means? Do you agree? How does her father's nature influence Miri and how she sees the world?

Note: These questions are keyed to Bloom's Taxonomy *as follows: Knowledge: 1–3; Comprehension: 4–5; Application: 6–7; Analysis: 8–10; Synthesis: 11–12; Evaluation: 13–14.*

Activities

1. When they return to the academy, the students must convince Tutor Olana that she must allow them new freedoms. Choose an issue or a belief that is important to you, and write an argument that will convince your classmates to agree.

2. Although Peder tells Miri that she does not need to sing to quarry-speak, she finds it helpful to maintain her concentration. Take some time to create your own form of quarry-speech. Is there a song connected to it? What is the memory that you'll use?

3. Draw a scene from the book—the girls lined up to meet the prince or, perhaps, the town working in the quarry. Be sure to use details from the story to help bring your picture to life.

Other Books by Shannon Hale

The Goose Girl
Enna Burning